CHAPTER 1

*"I*t is not a true romance if it does not have a happy ending."

Cassandra's bold statement was met with the expected chorus of opinions. In a room of women who are all passionate about their preferences in their romance novels and never hesitated to share their true thoughts, her view would not go unchallenged.

But she maintained her position as she sat in the center of the room and placed her hand over her heart as though making a lifelong vow.

Although she supposed in a way, she was.

"Why did we just put ourselves through such tragedy for entertainment?" she continued, her spine straight in her perch on the middle cushion of the crimson French sofa, which was beginning to show all of its decades. "I apologize, Faith, for I know the book was your choice, but I was so *invested* in their love, and then for it all to end in such a tortuous manner… I simply cannot go through that again."

"Cassandra," Faith said, tilting her head to study her friend. "You are being overly dramatic. It is still a romance because they fell in love. Yes, they allowed external forces to come between them, but the story is still worth reading. Did we not learn something from it?"

"We did," Cassandra said with a firm nod of her head. "Never trust a gentleman who is more in love with a ghost than his wife."

Persephone, who they affectionately called Percy, started to snicker at that, while Faith rolled her eyes. Faith's sister, Hope, sighed, and Cassandra knew that she likely agreed with her. The fair-haired, blue-eyed Hope lived up to her name, always seeing the best in everyone around her, while Faith was far more suspicious of anyone who entered her life.

One could tell their personalities by their choice in books – which made Cassandra all the more worried about what Madeline might pick the following week.

Percy held up a hand to halt a new argument.

"Before we delve deeper into this conversation, perhaps we should pour ourselves a drink."

"An excellent idea," Cassandra said, smiling wickedly as she walked to the sideboard, where her brother, Gideon, kept his alcohol. She had a feeling he knew that she and her friends often helped themselves to his supply, but each woman took a turn providing sustenance for their meetings so that there was never enough missing for him to have reason to accuse them.

She reached underneath and found five short glasses, lining them up in a row on the chipped wood of the counter above. She generously poured each one, and then served them to her friends before sitting back in her own place on the sofa, closing her eyes and taking a deep sip, welcoming the fiery warmth as it slid down her throat – just as the door opened, startling all of them.

"Gideon, I—oh, excuse me."

2

The deep, bass voice echoed through the room and straight into Cassandra's soul. It was a voice she knew well, one that she usually attempted to avoid.

For it brought nothing but trouble.

She shot to her feet so quickly that the remnants of her drink spilled out and splashed over her dress, but she disregarded that as she locked eyes with the dark, unreadable ones of the man in front of her – the man she had allowed to get under her skin, not to mention a few other places he should never have been – one too many times.

His broad, full lips curled into a smirk as his eyes wandered from her face down the entirety of her body to the kid slippers that covered her toes and back up again. His scrutiny was more fiery than the liquid that was dripping over her and she shivered from the intensity of it.

"Having ourselves a good time, are we ladies?" he asked, although he kept his eyes on Cassandra.

"We are having a private meeting," she said, straightening her shoulders and meeting his gaze full-on, refusing to cower before him. "One to which gentlemen are not invited. I believe Gideon is hosting a gathering of his own – one that you *are* likely welcome at – in the drawing room. This is the parlor."

"So it would seem," he said, his eyes sweeping around the room, missing nothing, including the books that each of them held in their laps. Cassandra gripped hers tightly in her hand as she moved it slightly behind her back so that he wouldn't comment upon it. She had nothing to fear from the man, she reminded herself. The worst he could do was tell Gideon what they were doing in here, and the truth was, she didn't think her brother would overly care.

"Lord Covington," Hope said belatedly, standing with a slight bow, one which they all followed – even Cassandra, as much as it aggravated her to do so.

3

She could tell he was completely aware of her feelings as his grin stretched wider and his eyes turned darker.

"Lady Cassandra," he replied, slipping his hand into his jacket and producing his handkerchief with a flourish, "I believe you might be in need of this."

Cassandra's hands balled into fists as she wanted to deny it – deny *him* – with everything within her. But she could feel the close gaze of her friends and she knew that she was best to simply take it from him and then hope he would leave.

"Thank you," she said through gritted teeth, crossing the room toward him and practically ripping it from his fingers before lifting it up to her body. Then she realized that two could play this game.

Ensuring that no one else in the room – except Lord Covington or Devon as she had always known him – could see her actions, she smiled coyly as she brought the handkerchief to her neck, slowly wiping away drops of the drink from her collarbones and then down to her cleavage. She dipped his handkerchief, noting it was embroidered with his initials, D.A., into the valley of her breasts, watching his nostrils flare as she did so.

She fixed an innocent look upon her face as she lifted the handkerchief and held it out toward him.

"Here you are," she said, annoyed by the breathy tone of her voice as she realized that her plan had unintended consequences when warmth washed over her, her teasing affecting her as much as she had meant to affect him.

His ungloved hands brushed against hers when he accepted it back, causing a most unwelcome tingle to rush up her arms and down her spine. He crushed the handkerchief in his hand as he nodded to her and then the rest of her friends before he turned on his heel and swiftly left the room.

THE EARL'S SECRET

RECKLESS ROGUES
BOOK ONE

ELLIE ST. CLAIR

Facebook: Ellie St. Clair

Cover by AJF Designs

Do you love historical romance? Receive access to a free ebook, as well as exclusive content such as giveaways, contests, freebies and advance notice of pre-orders through my mailing list!

Sign up here!

Reckless Rogues
The Earls's Secret
The Viscount's Code
Prequel, The Duke's Treasure, available in:
I Like Big Dukes and I Cannot Lie

For a full list of all of Ellie's books, please see
www.elliestclair.com/books.

Leaving quite the shocked air behind him.

Cassandra's shoulders stiffened for a moment, knowing what she would be facing when she turned around to her friends.

"Well," Percy said with wide eyes. "That was… interesting."

Madeline, the only one of the women who knew the full story of Cassandra's history with Devon, was wearing a knowing smile as she crossed her arms over her chest, waiting for Cassandra's response. Some help she was.

Cassandra cleared her throat.

"Shall we return to our discussion?"

Faith lifted a brow.

"Perhaps you should first tell us of what just transpired between you and the earl."

Cassandra should have expected this, although she wasn't entirely sure how to explain. Behind closed doors here in their book club room they were not the most proper of women, but they were still, for the most part, innocent young ladies who would be rather shocked if they knew the full truth.

"Lord Covington is my brother's closest friend," she said, lifting a hand as though it didn't mean anything.

"Of that we are aware," Faith said. "But I can hardly see how him being the friend of your brother could lead to such… tension."

Cassandra walked over to the sideboard and repoured her brandy before taking her seat, giving herself a moment to collect her thoughts by sipping from the glass.

"He and my brother spent much of their youth torturing me," she said, hoping her tone was nonchalant. "I have never been particularly pleased with the part he played in encouraging Gideon."

"How long did this *torture* last?" Percy asked, clearly understanding there was, perhaps, more to the story.

"It has never ended," Cassandra said, allowing her ire at the man to flow into her words. "Although I haven't seen him in some time. I have tended to avoid him since I... returned."

"Sometimes they say mocking is a form of flirtation," Hope said in her soft voice. "He could have a particular penchant for you."

"That is a lovely way to look at it, Hope, but I can assure you that he most certainly does not."

Hope shrugged as she took a small sip of her drink. Cassandra knew Hope would never admit to another soul outside of this room that she enjoyed it, preferring her lemonades when drinking in public. But then, she was as sweet of a woman as one could ever find and would never want to disturb her mother nor cause any discord.

"Lord Covington is nothing more than a nuisance, and a nuisance that I would prefer to avoid," Cassandra said, picking up her book to note to the rest of them that she was finished with their current conversation. "Now, can we discuss how much better this book would have been had the hero not been killed in the end?"

They seemed to accept her explanation – or at least respect her obvious preference to not discuss it any further – for now, at least. It wasn't until the women had concluded their book discussion for the day and departed, leaving just Madeline and Cassandra, that Cassandra knew she would have to face the truth.

"So tell me," Madeline said, as she settled back against the sofa, her brown eyes flashing in amusement as she looked at Cassandra impishly, "just what are you going to do about Lord Covington?"

"There is nothing *to do* about him," Cassandra said, walking around the room and collecting their glasses. Of course the maids would be in to clean, but Cassandra didn't want them knowing exactly what she and her friends were doing in here. It was one thing to discuss books that none of them were supposed to be reading, and quite something else for them to be drinking brandy while doing so.

Her mother was aware of their book club, but as far as she knew, they were reading *An Enquiry Into the Duties of the Female Sex* and discussing just how they should be conducting themselves in order to attract proper husbands.

"Cassandra, the moment he stepped into the room, the air was filled with an obvious edge," Madeline said. "Perhaps what was between you was never completely resolved."

"It *was*," Cassandra said with vehemence in her voice, more so to convince herself than Madeline. "It was a mistake. One that should never have happened."

"One that left you ruined."

"No one knows that."

"Except you. And him."

"What does it matter?" Cassandra asked, lifting her hands. "Only my mother and Gideon were aware that I made an immoral choice. Although they never discovered the full extent of it, they ensured I paid for it. No one else knows anything for certain, so therefore, no slight on my honor."

"The man you marry might find out."

"It would be too late by then," Cassandra said through gritted teeth, for it was a battle that she had fought within herself for far too long.

That was the very thing which had held her back from marriage – the knowledge that she would have to hide the truth from her husband until her wedding night, and once he found out, there was no consequence that could turn out in her favor.

It would hardly be a way to start a marriage, and for that reason, she had resisted for a long time. Of course, it had been rather difficult to explain to her mother just exactly *why* she had refused any suitor who showed interest in her.

She was the daughter of a duke, the sister of a marquess who would one day be one of the most powerful men in the country. And here she was, avoiding any gentleman interested in her.

"There is one other thing you are forgetting," Madeline said, lifting one of her dark eyebrows, with that expression that terrified most men, intimidating them from coming too close.

"Which is?"

"That you cannot help yourself from being attracted to him, that no other man has ever been good enough for you."

"That's not true," Cassandra said staunchly.

"It is," Madeline said, though her voice held nonchalance as though she had no desire to argue with Cassandra about it. "I don't understand why the two of you did not just marry and be done with it."

"Because we can hardly stand being in the same room together, let alone in front of an altar," Cassandra said. The truth was, she had barely spoken to Devon after... it... happened, as she had refused to allow him close to her once more. "And I could never trust him again," she finished softly.

She had told herself to move on, had assumed that she would in due time – that soon enough, another man would enter her life, one who was appropriate, who she could tolerate, who would be her friend and her husband.

But no other stirred her soul. Not like Devon had, even if it was not always in the way she would prefer.

She just had no idea what she was supposed to do about it.

CHAPTER 2

*D*evon's irritation grew when he had to take a moment to compose himself before he continued on to the drawing room to meet with Gideon and the rest of their society of gentlemen.

Damn Lady Cassandra Sutcliffe and the way she affected him.

From the moment he had laid eyes on her, when she was nothing more than a six-year-old, two years his junior, he had been drawn to her, although the feelings that accompanied that connection had changed over the years.

As he had grown into a young man, his confusion with his captivation of her had led to him teasing her mercilessly, convincing her brother to take part in his jokes and pranks.

In the meantime, she had grown into the most alluring woman he had ever laid eyes on. The only problem was that she had already learned to despise him with the same amount of passion he desired her. A passion that he yearned to unleash.

Which they had – once. All that had led to was guilt which had followed him around ever since, a coming

9

together that should have been the most magical of moments but instead had turned into a dirty secret.

A secret that he held deep within him, not sharing with anyone – not even Gideon, the closest friend he had in the world.

For Gideon would see his actions as the ultimate betrayal, and Devon had promised Cassandra he would keep their tryst between them.

Devon had tried to do the right thing, truly he had, but she had refused to even speak with him, let alone listen to reason. And in the end, she was likely right. He wouldn't have wanted to spend his life with a woman who had only married him because she had no other choice.

Except... he had never been able to rid her from his mind, and no other woman had been able to fill that place in his head and his heart, for she had taken up that space, just as stubborn there as she was in truth, refusing to make room for anyone else.

So he did what any man would do – he avoided her as best he could. It had been simple when she had been away, staying with family, but now it wasn't always easy when she lived in the same house as his closest friend.

He took a breath, pushing her from his thoughts as he walked into the drawing room, finding the other four men already waiting for him.

"Gentlemen," he greeted them. They looked up at him from their places around the room. They didn't often meet here – the drawing room was more women's territory and they preferred a room at their club – but Gideon had told them that he had reason for them all to meet in private instead.

"Covington, I wasn't sure you would ever arrive," Gideon said, his large frame rather out of place in his mother's dainty pink chair.

"I was waylaid when I entered the parlor instead," he said, "where I found your sister and her friends."

Gideon waved a hand in the air. "They are always in there, reading books on etiquette and how to find a husband or something of the like."

"I see," Devon said, although he couldn't help his smirk, for he had seen what they were reading – and it was no book on etiquette, although he supposed that there was something to be learned about catching a husband in a book such as what they'd had in front of them – or, in Cassandra's case, that she had been attempting to hide behind her back.

He met Gideon's eye, realized that Cassandra's brother knew exactly what they were up to in there, and with a nod so slight that none of the rest of them would notice, he let the subject matter lie.

Gideon had been there for him in more ways than he could count – including helping him out of a few impossible situations when they had been up to their pranks at Eton. Devon had much more propensity for being caught.

"So, what is the latest suggestion?" Devon asked, pouring himself a drink – wondering if it was the same brandy that Cassandra had been wiping off her delectable bosom, little minx – as he waited for Gideon's latest scheme. The five of them had come together at school out of boredom, more than anything. Boredom with the life in front of them, seeking more, thrills that they couldn't find elsewhere.

It would have been as frowned upon as Cassandra's little book club would be, but in their case, if they were to be discovered, they would be forgiven. That was the difference in being a man versus a woman in this part of society. But there was nothing that Devon could do about it but accept it.

"Perhaps we should do something to slight Robertson again," Anthony Davenport, Viscount Whitehall, suggested gruffly. "I hate that man."

"I know you do, Whitehall," Gideon said. "But there will be time for that later."

"What about a prank that would have everyone talking?" Eric Rowley, Lord Ferrington, suggested. "Perhaps dressing up one of the statues on Temple Bar. Throw some pauper's clothes on King Charles the first."

His brother, Noah Rowley, was already shaking his head. "That would be seen as a political statement, not as a prank. It could lead to great misunderstanding."

"You do know how to take the fun out of such things," Ferrington said with a sigh, but Rowley just shrugged.

"'Tis the truth."

"Actually," Gideon – who was the Marquess of Ashford and would, in the future, become the Duke of Sheffield, said, "we are doing none of those things."

"Whyever not?" Ferrington asked with a frown.

"Because I have stumbled across something that is much more interesting. Something which would be of great interest to me and to my family – and that I would share with you."

That piqued the attention of the rest of them.

"Do get to your point, Ashford," Devon said. "You are enjoying the suspense of this far too much."

"Perhaps that is true," Gideon said with a small smile. "But I must take some joy from it. As most of you know, my father's illness has left our family in difficult circumstances."

Devon nodded, even though he was surprised that Gideon had mentioned it. They all knew it to be true, but it was not something that the family often spoke of. Gideon's father, the current duke, was in the country, an invalid, while Gideon looked after his duties and made all decisions. When Gideon was a boy, the responsibilities had been entrusted to stewards and men-of-business, but a leader had been needed at the helm. Gideon had always been the responsible one, using this club of theirs and their activities as a release. But at his heart, he was a man who took care of everyone else – most especially his family.

He had just been too young and naive to save the estate from being mismanaged and the coffers from being emptied. He was doing all he could to build it back up – a fact that Devon admired, but he hoped it wasn't too little too late.

"I have found something that could restore our family fortunes," Gideon said, a rare grin widening across his face. "We do, however, have to work for it."

"I'm not following," Devon said with a frown, and Gideon held up a finger and continued as the rest of them leaned forward in interest.

"I was in my study last night, and my letter opener fell to the back of the drawer," Gideon said, acting out what had occurred as he described it. "I reached for it but couldn't find it anywhere. I pulled out the drawer to see if the opener had become lodged in the side, and I was right – it had. But when I pulled it out, something else happened that I wasn't expecting."

"You are enjoying this storytelling far too much," Devon said wryly, although he couldn't help but be the one to ask, "What was it?"

"The bottom of the drawer fell out," Gideon said, his blue eyes, so like his sister's, a rather unfortunate fact, lighting up as he said it. "There was a secret compartment attached to the bottom. Not overly large, just enough to fit a slip of paper."

They were silent as they waited for Gideon to continue.

"Well?" Devon demanded, "tell us what was in there, man."

"It was a riddle," Gideon said. "One that, from what I can tell, leads to a fortune."

They all stared at him with gaping mouths before looking

at one another. Devon scratched his head. Gideon was usually a reasonable man, but perhaps he had been pushed too far trying to restore his fortunes.

"Are you certain that is what it was?" Devon asked slowly.

"Yes," Gideon said, ire in his tone. "And before you doubt me, allow me to read it to you."

He carefully took a piece of paper out of a book on the table and cleared his throat before he began.

"*Oft surrounded by a deep, wet ditch, where flags fly and women stitch,*

Those of the house may never know,

A treasure of magnitude that does lie below.

Right before one goes to bed,

Where that one might set his head,

He guards what many would try to seek,

If worthy enough they will make themselves meek."

They were all silent for a moment as they pondered the words.

"Interesting," Rowley said, leaning forward. A learned, intelligent man who, as a second son, had always known he would have to find a way to support himself, tapped a finger against his lips. "Does it mean anything to you?"

"I suppose that the first line could reference a castle – which must mean Castleton, our country estate," Gideon said. "That desk has been in this house for years now – likely as far back as when my great-grandfather or great-great-grandfather was duke. The country estate has been entailed since then."

"True," Whitehall said, and Devon knew he would likely have an objection – he always seemed to. "But if it's a family fortune, why would one not simply leave it in a will or have it entailed to the estate? Why keep it secret and create some child's game to find it?"

"Perhaps one must be worthy to earn it," Ferrington said with a grin. "Do you think that man is you, Ashford?"

Gideon snorted, even though Devon knew him well enough to read him – he certainly did think he was the one who deserved to find it.

"If I can speak to my father in one of his more lucid moments, he might have some ideas," Gideon said. "Although I do not believe he would be up to solving a riddle."

The story told regarding the Duke of Ashford was that he had a wasting disease, but Devon knew the truth – he had an affliction to his mind, one that meant he had been kept away in order to prevent him from further damaging the family's reputation or fortunes. It was part of what had led to the Sutcliffes' initial downfall.

"What do *we* have to do with any of this?" Rowley asked.

"I thought perhaps that you might think on it a bit, see if all our minds together could come up with some answers for the mystery. In the meantime, I will be heading to the country soon. Perhaps there will be an opportunity for you to join me for a house party and we can spend some time searching together."

They nodded. It was always a rather grand time at Castleton Estate, even if they never held formal parties anymore.

Devon had one more question, however, one that he couldn't help but ask. "Will you tell your mother and your sister of this?"

"No," Gideon said swiftly. "You know what Cassandra is like. If she finds out about this, she will stop at nothing to find the answer herself – especially if she thinks it is some kind of competition she can best me in."

Devon had to hide his smile at that, for Gideon's words were true. Cassandra enjoyed nothing more than a good battle with her brother.

The five of them debated a few more of the lines before they all called it an afternoon and returned to their respective homes. As Devon was walking out the door, however, Gideon called him back and asked him to stay a moment.

"I have another favor to ask," Gideon said, and Devon nodded.

"Of course."

"Would you accompany me to Castleton when I go next week? An extra set of eyes wouldn't hurt."

"I don't see why not," Devon said after considering it for a moment. "I have nothing keeping me here at the moment, and my mother and sisters are in good hands with Spencer."

Devon might be the firstborn, but his brother had always been just as responsible, if not more so.

"Very good," Gideon said, relief crossing his face. "It shouldn't be for long. I might also need some help keeping Mother and Cassandra from knowing what we are doing. Our excuses would be more plausible if we are both there."

Devon paused. "They will be coming as well?"

"Of course," Gideon said, his brows forming a vee. "It gives them both time to see Father and with the season done, it makes sense to return anyway. Is that a problem? I know that you and Cassandra have never gotten on particularly well, but that was all in the past, was it not? You have barely seen her in years."

Because both Devon and Cassandra had made sure of it. But it was too late for excuses.

"Not a problem at all."

"Very well, then. Next week it shall be."

CHAPTER 3

Cassandra had known that Madeline's choice for their next book would be an odd one, and she was right. Some might consider it a romance, but Cassandra did not – at least, not yet. It read more like a crime novel, as it involved a mystery in which it seemed a wife had murdered her husband. She now had other interested suitors, but it was difficult to decipher just who was at fault and who was the love interest.

As they had selected their books months ago, Cassandra had perused the shelves of the library at their country estate to see if she could locate any of them before purchasing a copy, and this particular one had been sitting on the shelves, far at the back and nearly forgotten about. The books they chose were not meant for young ladies, and Cassandra had always wondered just why their library seemed to hold such books. One of her relatives must have held a similar interest, she thought with a chuckle.

Thinking of where she had found the book reminded Cassandra that they would return to visit the estate soon, according to Gideon. Cassandra was both looking forward to it and slightly apprehensive about it as well. For while she loved being out in the country, with the freshness of the air and the grounds around them, it was also always rather melancholy with the state of her father, which sometimes led to her mother's desolate moods as well.

She turned a page, surprised when a piece of paper fluttered out of the book and onto the cover of her bed where she was resting. It had obviously been there for some time, as it was rather thin and seemed fragile, and Cassandra picked it up with careful fingers.

"What do we have here?" she murmured, her eyes passing over it quickly.

"*Oft surrounded by a deep, wet ditch, where flags fly and women stitch,*" she read out loud, wondering as she did just what it could mean. Was it a poem?

She continued down to the next line, and the further she read, the wider her eyes grew. For it seemed, if she was not mistaken, that this was some kind of riddle. But what was it regarding? It was only when she reached the last line that the meaning of it all hit her. The riddle was leading the reader to a place, a place where the prize it referenced at the end could be found. A prize that, from the line *A treasure of magnitude that does lie below* seemed to be a rather significant one.

Oh, the possibilities. A great many things could be done with such a magnificent prize, she considered. It could buy her a life in which she could look after herself if she never married – which seemed like more of a reality with each passing day. But then, it could also go toward helping restore her family's fortunes to what they had been at one point in time. She had seen the look on her mother's face when she had wistfully run her hand over the finest fabrics in the store. It was not as though their family was destitute, but Cassandra knew how hard Gideon was working to look after them.

The first two lines were rather simple. She guessed that they would lead to a place within Castleton – it had to be. Just where, however, was another question entirely and one she couldn't seem to decipher – at least not quite yet.

The more she thought on it, the more excited she became – until she realized that she could be getting ahead of herself. What if this was nothing more than the page of another book? Or a poem written in the form of a riddle? And even if there was any truth to it, what were the chances that this treasure had not already been found, that it would actually be waiting for her?

She bit her lip as she shook her head, pushing away the thoughts. This paper had come to her for a reason, she considered, and if it wasn't for her to figure out, then who else could possibly do so?

She would have to think more on it in the morning, she decided, for she was too tired at the moment to properly decipher any more of it. Perhaps she would also bring it to her book club. Her friends were intelligent women. They were sure to have their own thoughts and fresh perspectives on the matter as well.

For a moment, Cassandra wondered whether she should go to Gideon with this right away. He would be interested, that was for certain, but then he would also likely take the riddle and the game from her and want her to have nothing more to do with it. She knew he thought he was looking out for her best interests, but he still treated her like a child who needed looking after, even though he was a mere two years older than she. Giving him this, something that actually intrigued her besides a story found within the pages of a book, was not an option – at least, not right now.

First, she would speak to her friends, and then, when she was ready, she would go to Gideon.

She would solve this riddle and do what she could for her family. She was certain of it.

* * *

CASSANDRA DIDN'T HAVE a chance to meet with her friends until the following week, on the day before her family was set to depart to Castleton. The estate was not particularly far, thank goodness, a day's journey away.

Still, they would likely be there for a time so there was much to prepare for. Cassandra was pleased, at least, that Hope and Faith would be at their own country home nearby as well and would be leaving shortly.

With her mother in quite the fuss with all of the preparations to be made before their departure, Cassandra suggested that they avoid her townhouse altogether and instead enjoy the day outside, taking advantage of the early spring weather. They walked through Hyde Park until they found a peaceful spot on the grass near the edge of the Serpentine and their maids spread out blankets for the ladies to sit and – ostensibly – discuss their books, although Cassandra had other plans in mind.

"Before we begin to consider the first few chapters of Madeline's book, I have something to share with you all," Cassandra said, too excited to even have poured their drinks yet. They might have been out of the house, but her basket contained a few surprises within it that would have been sure to shock anyone else from the *ton* walking nearby – if they were ever to discover their secret. "I have found a riddle that is going to lead us to treasure."

The women all looked at her as though she had gone mad, and Cassandra couldn't help but laugh.

"I thought the same myself when it first fell into my lap. However, I have had time to consider it, and there must be some truth to it. Perhaps there is no treasure, but there most certainly is a clue."

She had tucked the riddle back where she had found it, into the pages of the book, and she flipped through until it appeared once more.

"Here it is," she insisted, carefully holding up the letter to show all of them before turning it back around to read aloud. "I shall tell you what it says."

They all leaned in slightly, the better to hear, and Cassandra read the riddle aloud, line by line. By the time she was done, her friends were all watching her with rapt attention.

"What does it mean?" Hope asked breathlessly.

"I believe the first line is referencing Castleton, although I am unsure of the rest," Cassandra said truthfully. "I have spent far too much time over the past week attempting to decipher the words, but nothing makes sense. I am hoping that once I am at Castleton, it will begin to come together."

"It all sounds like some sort of fanciful game to me," said Faith, her nose up slightly in the air as though she was above the riddle. "Why would someone hide a treasure and then create a riddle to lead you there? It sounds like child's play. Where did you find it anyway?"

"Interestingly enough, in the pages of this very book I was reading. The book had been on the shelves at Castleton for years from the looks of it. When I knew our list for the season, I searched the library to see if we owned any of them."

"So someone wrote out a riddle that pointed the bearer to Castleton and then hid the clue in a random risqué book on the shelves? Why?"

Cassandra shrugged. "There are some mistakes in the spelling. Perhaps this was a first copy before another one was written?"

21

"And it somehow became stuck in the book?"

"Maybe the writer was in the middle of reading the book when she began anew."

"Why do you think the writer was a woman?" Percy asked, tilting her head to the side, one of her red-gold curls bobbing as she did so.

"The wording seems quite clever," Cassandra said, her lips curling into a smile. "Hardly creative enough for a man to have come up with."

Madeline snorted at that but seemed to agree.

"Well, I am pleased to have put this in motion, having been the one to select the book in which it was found. The writer of the riddle obviously had good taste," Madeline said with a grin. "Now, what are we to do with this?"

"As it happens, I will be leaving for Castleton soon – tomorrow, actually – and will begin searching. I was hoping that some of you might have ideas as to what the rest of the riddle is referencing."

"We will certainly try to think on it," Hope said, "although you know the estate better than anyone."

"Have you told your brother?" Madeline asked, arching one of her perfect eyebrows.

"No," Cassandra shook her head. "He would tell me that I shouldn't be involved in this, or he would feel that I was placing too much importance into it. I shall tell him once I have a better idea of whether anything will be found."

They nodded as they were silent for a moment, considering the mystery she had placed before them. As Cassandra had already spent so much time on trying to solve the clues, her gaze drifted out over the water before them. There were a few rowboats arching through the calm blue water that was practically sparkling with the sunshine of the day. A couple of the boats were moving rather leisurely, while another was slicing over the surface more quickly, as though he was part of Oxford's own racing team.

Cassandra squinted. There was something familiar about the way the rower moved. He almost reminded her of—then the boat slowed and the rower lifted a hand.

Oh goodness. It was not only *him*, but he had caught her watching him. She whipped her head around, pretending she hadn't seen him, that she hadn't been captivated by his speed, the way the muscles of his shoulders had bunched as he pulled back the oars, how she could imagine the strength of his thighs as they pushed against the bottom of the boat.

For even if she couldn't see them, she knew what they looked like, what they had felt like under her hands. Sometimes, she could still remember—

"Cassandra?"

Her face heated as she realized she had been caught in her reveries.

"Yes?" she answered Hope, having to clear her throat.

"Are you all right? You appear to be rather overcome. Do you think—"

"I'm fine," she said, shaking her head as she lifted a hand to fan her face. "It must be the weather, is all. It is rather warm, isn't it?"

"It is spring," Faith said, eyeing her, "but I would not say that the heat is anything unbearable. Are you sure you are well?"

"Of course," she assured her. "Why do I not fetch our drinks?"

She reached into the basket and found the decanter, passing them each a glass before she began to pour.

Percy took a sip and then coughed slightly.

"Goodness," she said. "That is rather strong."

"So it is," Cassandra agreed with a smile. "Is there any other way to drink brandy?"

She decided with her fist sip that she would push away all thoughts of a certain rower who refused to leave her mind. Damn Devon Addison. The now-Lord Covington was occupying far too many of her thoughts as of late.

She smiled at her friends, opening her mouth to ask them if any ideas had arisen – until she saw all of their eyes move to something over her shoulder. She turned to see what had so captured their attention, and her breath caught in her throat when she saw just who was standing behind her, those thighs she had pictured just above her head, his stance wide and hands on his hips as he looked down at her with that arrogant smile she wanted to reach up and wipe off his face, primarily because of what it did to her.

"A lovely day to sit outside, isn't it ladies?" he said, waving them away when they stood to bow before him – all but Cassandra. "Came out to watch some rowing, did you?"

"Oh, I didn't see anyone on the water," Hope said, turning around to look now, and Cassandra closed her eyes as she felt Devon's gaze on her. He had realized that it was her watching him, damn the man.

"No?" he said, and Cassandra refused to look at him, for she knew the self-important smirk he would be wearing. "I just came from the water myself and could have sworn that I had spectators."

He dropped to the ground beside Cassandra, sitting far closer than she would have liked. "If you are not here as observers, then just what are we doing on the banks of the Serpentine?"

He reached out a hand, and Cassandra snatched up her book before he could grasp it. True, she would prefer that he didn't see what she was reading, but she was even more worried that the riddle would fall out of the pages and into his hands. That would never do, for if he found such a thing he was certain to mention it to Gideon.

"*We* are reading," she said primly. "We decided to take our discussion out of doors today."

"Did you, now? And what has you all so captivated?"

"It is a book on etiquette, of course," Cassandra said. "That is what we prefer to read."

"Right," he said, obviously struggling to ensure that his face remained passive, his lips curling and uncurling.

Since he couldn't reach the book, instead he went for Cassandra's drink. She let out a small grunt of irritation while attempting to tug it from his grasp, but he was too strong for her, lifting it to his lips and taking a big swig. Cassandra watched him with her mouth agape.

"Why, Lady Cassandra," he said, his own eyes widening in shock as he sputtered just slightly. "That is… ah… fortifying."

He paused, putting the drink down, before he cleared his throat once more and then took another sip, although this time it was much smaller. She could but imagine that he had been expecting something else entirely to quench his thirst.

"I will say, you have excellent choice in quality," he said with a wink, and Cassandra was both annoyed and aroused at the same time. "Are you looking forward to leaving London for Castleton?" he asked.

She nodded. "Yes, I suppose I am."

"As am I," he said, smiling.

It took Cassandra a moment to realize exactly what he was saying. "Pardon me?"

"I have the great fortune to be accompanying you for a time," he said, his grin stretching wider as though he knew how she would accept the news and was glad of it. "It is always a wonderful place to be at this time of year, isn't it?"

"But—" she began to protest, only there was nothing for her to say. If Gideon had invited him, then who was she to deny her brother's choice in companion? She let out a sigh that was obviously more audible than she had intended, for she could sense Madeline's sharp gaze upon her. "But I do love the summer as well," she finished lamely, unable to come up with anything more clever. "I'm sure it will be a lovely stay overall."

He grabbed an apple from her basket, his teeth crunching into it as he stood. "I look forward to it," he said with that wink again, and Cassandra had to take a breath to try to calm herself.

"Ladies." He nodded to the rest of them before walking away, and Cassandra had to force her eyes away from him and back toward her friends.

"Well," Faith said. "So much for ambivalence."

Perhaps Castleton was not going to be as relaxing as Cassandra had originally thought.

CHAPTER 4

*D*evon chuckled to himself as he wandered down the hallway to meet with Gideon. He was going to have far too much fun annoying Lady Cassandra with his presence here at Castleton. He hadn't seen much of her on the journey here, for he and Gideon had ridden beside the carriage that held Cassandra and her mother. They had arrived late enough in the evening that the women had taken their meals in their rooms before retiring for the night.

He had caught glimpses of her, of course, especially when they had stopped to lunch, but she was so preoccupied with glaring at him that it was difficult to actually speak to her. He had considered asking Gideon for advice on how to melt her icy exterior, but he knew his friend would surely wonder why he cared so much what Cassandra thought of him.

That was an explanation Devon was not inclined to provide.

He knocked quickly on Gideon's study door before letting himself in. He considered the man as close to him as his own brother was. Not only had their families spent a great deal of time together when they were children, their mothers being close friends, but Gideon and Devon being of the same age, they spent all of their years at school together, accompanying one another nearly wherever they went.

Gideon had been reserved as a youth, and Devon had been the one to speak for him for so long, eventually learning how to bring him out of the dark places Gideon would go into, where he would try to hide from the world that was asking too much of him at such a young age.

Gideon may be a man now, but it was one of the reasons that he could never find out what had happened between Devon and his sister. He would feel so betrayed – and rightly so.

"Devon," Gideon said, waving him into the room. He was standing at the sideboard, pouring a drink, and Devon couldn't help but be reminded of the drinks Cassandra had poured just two days ago while sitting on the banks of the Serpentine. As he had been rowing, he had felt eyes on him, and knew even before turning around that it had been her. He could sense her, no matter who else was near them or what else was happening – even from across the park, that connection had held true.

Not that she would ever admit it. He wished he knew why she hated him so, especially when she had been as eager as he that night and he had thought everything had changed. How wrong he had been.

"Are you comfortable in your chamber?" Gideon asked him, to which Devon nodded as he accepted the drink.

"Of course," he said. "I will always feel at home at Castleton."

"It is not what it used to be," Gideon said, shaking his head, which Devon understood. Gideon had been unable to make repairs to the estate for years, and the staff was not as hearty as it had been in the past. Yet, they did what they could, and the place was still clean and comfortable. Gideon and his mother had made sure that their country home – and the duke's permanent residence – was everything that it could be based on what they were able to provide.

"It is a wonderful place to stay now and will be as majestic as it ever was very soon," Devon assured him. "You have worked hard to return the Ashford name to its earlier fortunes."

"But will it ever be enough?" Gideon murmured. "I do not know if I can right everything."

"You are doing more than most other men would do," Devon said. "Do not be so hard on yourself."

Gideon nodded, even though Devon knew he likely wouldn't listen to his words. It was Gideon's way – he never thought he was good enough.

"Now," Devon continued, wanting to change the direction of the conversation and give Gideon something else to focus on, "what is our plan for this riddle?"

"If we were to solve it, perhaps it could restore our fortunes," Gideon said, brightening somewhat, and Devon nodded, although as much as he wanted to provide Gideon with some hope, he also didn't want those same hopes to be dashed if this all came to nothing.

"It will be an amusement, if nothing else," Devon said cheerily. "The first lines have led us here. What about the next lines?"

Gideon began to murmur them once more, obviously having committed them to memory.

"Those of the house may never know,
A treasure of magnitude that does lie below.
Right before one goes to bed,
Where that one might set his head,

He guards what many would try to seek,
If worthy enough they will make themselves meek."

Gideon frowned as he shook his head. "I have been over them time and again, and it could be so many places. Out of doors, perhaps, or in the servants' quarters? That would be a strange place to hide treasure, but then, sometimes what you are looking for is right in front of you."

"It is, isn't it?" Devon said, trying not to think of Cassandra. "What of the last lines that mention the treasure itself?"

"I haven't come up with anything based on the words, but for something of value to be so hidden, I would guess it must be jewels or coins, would it not? What else could be easily hidden?"

"That is a good guess," Devon murmured, although he considered that an eccentric ancestor might have had much different ideas about what could hold such value. "I was thinking—"

He stopped when he heard a thump on the other side of the door. He lowered his voice. "Did you hear that?"

Gideon's brow furrowed. "I did."

Devon jerked his head toward the door, not saying anything else for fear of giving away that he had heard the sound and alerting the culprit. He took slow, careful steps toward the entry, stopping just in front of it. He placed his hand on the doorknob, paused, and then wrenched the door open quickly.

Only to have a bundle of skirts, woman, and trouble fall right on top of him.

He caught Cassandra before she fell to the floor, taking full advantage of the opportunity to hold her in his arms once more.

Of course, she quickly batted his hands away, all hellfire and fury as her fists came to her hips and she glared at first him and then her brother.

"Cassandra," Gideon said from across the room, some surprise in his voice. "Just what do you think you are doing?"

"That's a question I might ask you," she said, fixing him with her stare. "How did you know?"

"Know what?"

"About the riddle!" she said, as if it should be obvious. "Did my maid find out and say something? Or did you—" she rounded and pointed a finger into Devon's chest, "—learn what we were doing when you found us near the Serpentine? I should have known that you would have listened in on our conversation."

"As you were doing right this moment?" Devon asked, arching one of his own brows, to which her cheeks turned a healthy shade of pink in answer, although she obviously was not going to apologize for anything.

"That's different," she countered instead.

"I fail to see how."

"I am in my own home. I was wandering down the hallway, minding my own business, when I heard the two of you speak a very familiar line – a line from a riddle I have in my possession. Of course I stopped to listen to determine just how you might have come across it."

"While I should never have greeted you and your friends after you were watching me row?"

"No, you shouldn't have! And I wasn't *watching* you. I was simply appreciating the beauty of the water."

"Of course," Devon said, unable to help the smirk that crossed his face. Damn, there was no other like this woman. She was a hellcat, and he loved it.

"That's enough," Gideon said, taking slow, measured steps toward him, and Devon was instantly ashamed, uncertain of whether Gideon had sensed the tension between them or was simply reacting to the freely flowing words.

It was actually a good thing Gideon was here, or Devon

might have found another way to quiet Cassandra – one that her brother was certain to not approve of.

"As it happens, Cass, I found the riddle myself," Gideon said. "It was hidden in a false bottom of one of the drawers of my desk back in London."

"In actuality?" she asked, her eyes instantly suspicious, and Devon wondered just who had hurt her to such an extent that it would cause her to never believe the truth, even if it came from her brother.

"What reason would I have to lie to you?" Gideon asked. "Of course it is the truth. I determined that the first line was leading us to Castleton. The rest I am uncertain about. I asked Devon to accompany us here to help me determine the next clue."

Cassandra crossed her arms over her chest. "Why didn't you say anything to me about it?"

"Well, it appears that you had the same thought in mind, if you were also in possession of the riddle and never mentioned it to your brother, who will one day actually own this estate and all that surrounds it," Gideon said wryly. "Come, sit, and tell us what you know."

Cassandra's arms and shoulders fell, finally giving in, as she and Devon took the chairs in front of Gideon's desk. "Very well," she said begrudgingly, and Devon couldn't help but smile at her show of emotion. She reached into a pocket within her gown and pulled out a book – not the one she had been reading the other day, he noted, but one that was rather nondescript, and opened it to reveal the page hidden within. "I found this in a book I was reading – one that I had brought to London from Castleton. We will have to compare copies, but it appears to be a first draft, with some spelling errors."

She held it out toward Gideon, and he placed it on his tidy desk so that they all could see it, before he pulled out his own riddle and set it beside to compare the two. Once they had all finished, they sat back and looked at one another in amazement.

"It appears you are right," Gideon said. "All has been corrected on my copy."

"Interesting," Cassandra murmured, her eyes lighting up, and Devon knew how much she was likely enjoying this. "So it was meant to be found in London."

"Why did you not tell me about your discovery?" Gideon asked, crossing one leg over the other as he sat back and waited for Cassandra.

"Because I thought you would not allow me to search for the clues any longer, that you would take it all away from me."

Gideon tilted his head as he considered her words. "You are likely right," he said. "I do not want you to trouble yourself with something like this. Devon is here, and he can help. Meanwhile you—"

"Can sit around and do needlework and paint watercolors of the grounds all day?" she said.

When Gideon's face colored slightly, Devon had to cover his laugh with a cough, for Cassandra had obviously been right as to his line of thought.

"I think not," she answered herself. "I would like to be part of this. It is the most interesting thing that will have happened to me in years."

"I'm not sure, Cassandra," Gideon said, shaking his head. "I don't like the thought of you traipsing all over the estate by yourself, searching out a mysterious treasure from a bewildering clue."

"What trouble could I possibly find in my own home?" she asked, splaying her hands out.

Even Devon would have considered that she had a fair point, although it wasn't for him to interject and say so.

"Besides, I would have been doing it alone anyway. At

least now, you will have an inkling of my actions and we can work together."

Gideon drew a breath, and Devon could tell by the defeat on his face that he had decided to give in. "Fine," he said. "You can help."

A satisfied smile spread across Cassandra's face, even though Devon was aware that she would have searched for the answer to the riddle whether or not Gideon had given his permission.

"There is just one thing," Gideon continued. "Something that I was actually going to speak with you about this morning, Devon."

Devon arched an eyebrow as he waited for his friend to continue.

"I know this is rather unfortunate timing, especially since we have just arrived. Trust me, I am not interested in making another journey so soon. However, I received a note this morning. There are some issues at one of our other properties nearby. It seems the steward has not been as diligent as he should have been, and I must go put all to rights. In fact, I might just sell the thing, we shall see, although I do not want to show any signs of weakness. I shouldn't be long, but while I am gone, Devon, would you mind staying a short time and looking after Cassandra and Mother? I know it is much to ask as you have your own responsibilities to care for, but it would be of great help for a short time."

Devon could feel Cassandra's horrified gaze turn to first her brother and then to him.

"Oh, Gideon, we shall be fine," she said hurriedly. "There is no need for Lord Covington to—"

"Of course," Devon interjected, leaning forward in his seat, enjoying this turn of events, as much as he would miss his friend's company. "I would be most happy to."

This was becoming more interesting by the moment.

34

And he wasn't going to waste his time alone with the lovely Lady Cassandra.

Oh no, he was going to prove to her once and for all that he was not the monster she considered him to be.

Just how he was going to do so was all that remained to be seen.

CHAPTER 5

*assandra left Gideon's study slightly shaken. Stay alone at Castleton with Devon? Well, she supposed she wasn't *entirely* alone. Both of her parents were here, but it was not as though her mother would have any inkling about why Cassandra wouldn't want to spend time with Devon, and she wasn't about to tell her.

Of course, Cassandra could insist that she must be properly chaperoned at all times, but that would certainly raise suspicions, especially as Devon was seen as practically part of the family and Cassandra had always been more likely to circumvent her supervision.

She would just have to continue her search as best she could while avoiding him, she reasoned. What else was she supposed to do?

Before anything else, she would pay a visit to her father, she decided. She missed him, truly she did, although it was always rather daunting to visit as she was never entirely sure just who would be greeting her when she walked into his room – the man who loved her and would do anything for her, the man who was so deep in his own demons that he could barely acknowledge anyone was there, or the man who was thrilled to see her but thought she was someone else entirely?

She steeled her shoulders and placed her hand on the banister to begin walking upstairs when she sensed a presence behind her. She turned to find Gideon there.

"Why do we not go together?" he asked softly, and she nodded, grateful for her brother and the relationship they had developed over the past few years. He allowed her to lead but was a solid presence at her back.

They greeted their father's valet at the door. In actual fact, he was part valet and part caretaker, and had forever been loyal to the family.

"Anderson," Gideon said. "How are you?"

"I am well, my lord," said the man who was roughly the same age as their father, although he appeared ten years younger. "It is good to see you."

"It is good to be back, although I wish it were for longer. Hopefully, upon my return I can stay for a greater amount of time. How is Father?"

"He is the same as ever, for the most part," Anderson said. "Today is a particularly good day, my lord, my lady. Your mother spent most of the morning with him, which, of course, raised his spirits dramatically, as it always does. I am sure he will be ever so pleased to see you."

"Thank you, Anderson," Cassandra said before they entered the room, which was as pleasant of a sick room one could ever come across.

The windows were open, allowing in the fresh spring air, the light curtains billowing with them, while the bed was turned so that their father could see outside. When the weather was mild, Anderson was keen to accompany him out of doors whenever possible.

And there, in the middle of the room, was their father.

He turned when he heard the door open, surprise lighting his face upon seeing them.

"There you are! George and Eve!"

Cassandra and Gideon shared a look. It was one of those days, then, when he confused them with his brother and sister. They had been through this a time or two, and while it always saddened Cassandra with a pang in her chest, she found it best to humor him instead of attempting to correct him, which only served to further confuse him.

"It's good to see you," she said instead, walking over and taking one of his hands between the two of hers. "How are you?"

"Very good, very good," he said. "Waiting for the weather to turn so that I can get out and visit the land."

"Of course," she said with a nod. Her father had always hated London, loving instead to work with the farmers and the land they owned in the area. It was partially why they had decided it was best for him to remain here in the country. "Did you see—" she was about to say 'Mother' but then realized it was likely best she continue on with his own line of thought, "Annabelle?"

"Yes, certainly," he said, looking at her quizzically. "She was here just this morning. Likely gone on to prepare herself for our ride."

"That's wonderful," Cassandra said. She walked over to the window, looking out at the lands stretching before them as Gideon began speaking with her father a bit more.

"I do have one more question," Gideon said just before they prepared to leave. They would see their father often in the country, as he would join them for dinner whenever he was having a particularly good day.

"Of course."

"Would you be interested in helping us solve a riddle?"

Cassandra shot a questioning look at her brother,

wondering if they should be mentioning this, but Gideon slightly nodded in response as their father's eyes lit up.

"How intriguing," their father said. "Do tell me more."

"Very well," Gideon said, before lowering his voice slightly and reciting him the lines of the riddle, lines that Cassandra realized both she and Gideon had memorized at this point. "Do those mean anything to you?"

Her father pursed his lips, tapping a finger against them as he turned and walked around the room in thought.

"I would guess the treasure is a piece of jewellery. Or a set, such as the one Mother used to wear."

"Did she?" Cassandra said, the idea of it piquing her interest. Perhaps her grandmother had been the one to write the riddle.

"She did," her father nodded. "She had an entire set of rubies, actually, handed down to her from her own mother. Our grandmother had royal blood, you know."

"I didn't know that," Cassandra said, exchanging a look with Gideon, who also shrugged. Apparently, it had not been part of family knowledge.

"Come, Eve, how could you not? You know she was from Spain, one of the younger daughters. Was married off to an English duke in expectation of peace or some sort," he said. "When she came to England, she brought with her this elaborate set of jewels. I always wondered what happened to it." He turned suddenly, his gaze piercing Cassandra. "Do you not have it?"

"Me?" she said. "Why on earth would I have it?"

"Probably because you are his sister," Gideon murmured in her ear, and Cassandra nodded slowly.

"Right," she said. "I meant, why do you think they are in my possession?"

"They are said to have disappeared one night from Grandmother's room. I assumed you had taken them, for you always had such an eye for them and were so angry when I told you that I was going to give them to my bride one day. It only makes sense."

"I understand why you would feel that way," Cassandra said slowly. "However, they are, unfortunately, not in my possession. But perhaps we can find them together."

"We shall certainly try," Gideon said. "Well, we must be going but will return soon. Good day, Fa—Your Grace."

"Good day," their father said, before Cassandra followed Gideon out the door and they said their farewells to Anderson.

"What was that about?" Cassandra asked as they continued down the stairs. "I agree the jewels could be the treasure that awaits, but it doesn't really matter if we do not know how to find them, now does it?"

"Do you truly think our aunt could have taken them?"

"I suppose anything is a possibility, although she would never admit it if she did," Gideon said.

"Nor could she ever wear them in public."

"But if they are worth as much as it appears they are, perhaps she could have sold them."

"Perhaps. We haven't seen her in so long."

"No," Gideon shook his head. "She far prefers Bath to London, and we have not ventured that way in some time. Perhaps we shall have to make a trip there soon, if we do not find what we are looking for. In the meantime, why do you not write her and ask what she knows of them? Now, it is time for me to depart as there are a few things that I really must take care of. Be careful, Cassandra, promise me that? And do allow Devon to help you. I know the two of you have not always got on well, but I trust him more than any other man. He would never let me down."

Cassandra doubted Gideon would say the same if he knew the truth of their past.

"Very well. Thank you, Gideon, and best of luck."

He patted her rather awkwardly on the shoulder before leaving for the study. Without his presence, Cassandra allowed the emotion of seeing her father to fill her, her shoulders falling as she wished that he was not as ill in the mind as he was, that he would see her and know her, as Cassandra, his daughter.

But all she could do was be grateful she still had the opportunity to be in his presence, she decided, as she turned toward the other side of the staircase to take some time alone in her bedchamber.

Until a figure emerged from the shadows, his arms behind his back and concern over his face.

She lifted her shoulders, putting her armor back on.

"Lurking again, are we?" she asked.

"Actually, no, not this time," Devon said, shaking his head as he took slow steps toward her, as though he considered her prey he was worried that he might scare away. He wouldn't be far from the truth, except that Cassandra was not the type of woman who would ever back down, no matter what she faced. "I had a question to ask Gideon before he left, but then I saw the two of you emerge from your father's room. You looked like you could use a friendly face."

"So then why would you provide me yours?" She regretted the words as soon as they left her lips, knowing that he was merely trying to be kind, but she was unable to help herself. This was Devon. The man she had allowed in, which had then led to her entire life veering off course.

"Cassandra," he said, looking at her in supplication. "When have I not been kind to you?"

Cassandra didn't know if there was any way to further express her incredulity with him than she had already attempted.

"When have you not been kind? Was it when you placed a toad in my bed? When you convinced my governess that I was the one playing practical jokes to try to be rid of her? When you offered to take me rowing and ended up depositing me in the pond? Or when we—when you—"

She stopped, unable to say the words aloud, especially when he was staring at her with such intensity in his dark brown eyes. She remembered what those eyes had looked like when his body was flush against hers, when he—actually, come to think of it, they looked rather like they did right now. She hurriedly stepped back.

"I thought I was most *kind* during that time," he said in a low voice, and she allowed him to feel the full extent of her glare.

"I thought so at the time as well. Until afterward," she said, and he tilted his head to the side.

"Is there something you are not telling me?" he said, concern causing his shoulders to rise, his voice to drop, his body to tense. "You had said there were no consequences. I thought—"

"There was no consequence as in no babe. In that, you are correct," she said, stepping back once more, having no wish to speak of this any further. "There was nothing for you to concern yourself with."

"I feel as though I have done something wrong, anyway," he said, lifting a hand toward her, dropping it when he realized there was no point in offering it.

"Nothing to worry yourself over," she murmured, turning her head away, hoping he wouldn't see the anguish in her eyes.

"Be that as it may, I am still worried," he said, closing the distance between them once more until they were but a foot apart. "I am trying to make it up to you, Cassandra, truly I am. Allow me in, tell me what you are feeling."

That, she couldn't do. She would never. For to reveal any vulnerable part of herself would be giving him far too much power.

"It makes perfect sense that I would feel some sadness after visiting my father, for he is unwell," she said. "Now, why do you not go and give Gideon a shoulder to cry on? He is the reason you are here, is he not?"

"He did invite me here, although now I am here to watch over you," he said. "So watching over you is what I am doing."

He tilted his head down toward her, and for a moment, Cassandra felt the familiar tingle that began in her toes and was readying itself to race upward. Fortunately, her head prevailed, and she stepped back just in time.

"I am not a child, Lord Covington."

"Oh, believe me, Cassandra, I would never confuse that."

Heat stole up her cheeks at what he was insinuating, and she stiffened her shoulders.

"I am walking away now. Please let me alone."

Did he actually look disappointed? Upset?

"Very well," he said, setting his chin. "If you need me, you know where to find me."

"I can assure you that I won't."

CHAPTER 6

*D*evon watched Cassandra walk away from him, her head held high, back as regally straight as any queen.

And wondered again just what had turned her into this jaded woman. It couldn't have been him... could it? What had she meant when she had said that there were *other* consequences? She had confirmed there was no baby, it being her sole response to him after it all had occurred those few years ago. They would have had no choice but to marry then, of course, despite her objections. Yes, they had both been rather young, but he had been a man in love, even though he realized much later it was more likely infatuation.

Perhaps Gideon could shed some light on the subject, though Devon would have to dance around just why he was interested in such a topic. He still had to speak with Gideon before he departed.

When he turned around to find him, however, he nearly walked right into another person.

"Your Grace," he said, bowing before the duchess, and she smiled as she regarded him.

"Lord Covington, it is lovely to have you here. I trust you are comfortable?"

"Of course," he said, noting how similar the exchange was to that with Gideon. He had a feeling both mother and son were rather worried about how their home would be regarded with their inability to do much upkeep besides the necessities. "I always feel very welcome at Castleton."

"I am glad to hear it," she said. "We have done all we can to make it home."

A flash of sadness passed over her face, one that he well understood. The duke and duchess had been a love match. He couldn't imagine what it must be like for her to have the person she loved be so close, so present, yet so far as well.

"I am glad to hear that you have chosen to stay on with us even as Gideon has been called away," she continued. "I am sure he will be back shortly, and in the meantime, Cassandra will be happy for the company. You have always been like family to us."

He nodded stiffly at her words, which contained far more meaning to him than she ever could have imagined.

"Thank you, Your Grace," he said, before he continued on his way to find Gideon, hoping he still had time to speak to him before he left.

He did appreciate the duchess' kind words. Devon had lost his father just over a year prior. While his mother had never been particularly warm to her children, he always found a duchess who actually spent time with her family to be an anomaly that he enjoyed.

After searching more than a few rooms for Gideon, he asked the passing housekeeper of his whereabouts and she suggested that he could be found in the stables. Devon dashed out, surprised to find that his friend was already preparing to depart.

"Leaving so soon?" Devon asked, and Gideon turned to

him, nodding.

"I am hoping that if I leave now, I can reach the estate before nightfall. Then, I should be able to take care of my business and return shortly."

"Take your time. All will be fine here," Devon assured him.

"I appreciate that, but even so, I am looking forward to returning and helping in the ," Gideon said with a self-depre-cating smile. "This is the most exciting thing that has happened to me in some time."

"That, I can understand," Devon said. "I wanted to ask, if you had remained here to search, where would you begin?"

Gideon cocked his head to the side as he considered it. "I would say the gardens. I know Cassandra believes the servants' quarters is the place to start, but I think she's wrong. It is too sparse, and the staff change over too often for a treasure not to be noticed. It would have been discov-ered by now. The gardens it is, in my opinion. It would be easy to hide something within them, and there are so many permanent statues and ornamental pieces, if you search there, you might turn up something."

"I shall do my best."

"Do not forget to at least keep up the pretense of including Cassandra," Gideon added. "It would be better that you keep her close than have her traipsing around by herself. You know the trouble she gets herself into."

"I do indeed."

More than anyone else would ever realize.

"Speaking of Cassandra," he said, lifting a finger, but Gideon had already began a conversation with the stable-master. By the time he turned around, he seemed to have something else on his mind.

"One last thing," Gideon said, holding onto his horse's reins. "Do be easy on Cassandra. I know she isn't always agreeable, but she's had a hard time since the… incident. Good luck, and I shall see you soon."

With that, he mounted his horse, and before Devon could fully grasp Gideon's departing words, he was riding away. By then it was far too late for him to follow or call him back to ask him to explain just what he was talking about. Incident? Whatever could he mean?

He supposed there was but one thing to do about it. He was going to have to ask Cassandra himself.

The only problem was, he didn't seem to be able to find any time to speak to her alone.

Her parents were both present at dinner that night, although the duke seemed to be of the belief that Cassandra was his sister, Eve, and Devon was her husband. As much as he could see the hurt on Cassandra's face that her father was not, in the moment, aware of her true identity, Devon decided that if he had to play a role, the role of her husband was not a particularly difficult one.

He pulled out her chair for her, allowing his fingers to skim over the soft, pale skin of her neck as he stepped back and away. She bristled, fixing him with a glare, but he simply smiled at her, knowing that doing so would likely vex her but uncaring at the moment.

"Good to see you here in the country, Robert," the duke said with a wide smile for him, and Devon could understand the family's sense of loss. For the duke was an upright man, one with a good heart who loved his family and had done his very best until life presented him with a challenge that he couldn't quite overcome.

All that had happened afterward was the fault of whatever sickness had struck him, not the duke's own intentions.

"I was thinking that perhaps tomorrow we should go check on the lands, Robert, what do you say? It could be like old times, riding together across the fields."

Devon stole a glance at Cassandra. He wouldn't mind accompanying the duke, but he wasn't sure that the man often ventured beyond the grounds, especially to speak to farmers and tenants.

"De—Robert and I are busy tomorrow, unfortunately, Father," Cassandra said gently, and Devon stirred to life when Cassandra reached over and placed her hand on his arm. She obviously noticed his reaction, for she pulled it back just as quickly. "Perhaps we can do something else together – within the house."

"I've been in this house for far too long," he grumbled. "I've just overcome my case of the grippe. Time to return outdoors."

"Must be a sign," Devon murmured, and Cassandra fixed him with a look, clearly misunderstanding him, but he found it interesting her father was also interested in leaving the house – although for an entirely different reason. Fortunately, no one else heard Devon's mutterings, for he didn't wish to explain their treasure , even though Gideon had told him that the duke was already aware they had a riddle to solve. It would be easier to continue on his own.

"So, are you newlyweds ready to add more members to the family?" the duke asked, causing Cassandra to choke on her drink while her mother admonished, "Gregory!"

He laughed away the question with a wave of his hand. "Eve doesn't mind such talk, do you, Eve?"

"I suppose not," Cassandra said, although Devon noticed that she couldn't meet his eye.

Devon took advantage of the situation and leaned back, lifting his arm and setting it on the back of her chair. She bristled slightly, although she didn't move away – likely for no more than the benefit of the charade they were putting on for her father.

"I am a fortunate man, to have married her," Devon said,

48

his lips curling up slightly into a smile, especially when Cassandra gripped his leg underneath the table, which did not have what he was certain was her desired intent but in fact just made him more eager to continue on his current path. "I am ever so grateful."

"You should be," she said with a frosty glare. "Being married to me is a great privilege."

"To which, I completely agree," he said, lifting his glass and holding it up to her. She ignored him for a moment, until her mother hissed, "Cassandra," and she sighed before clinking hers ever so slightly against his.

Devon smiled as he figured he had won this battle. But he was smart enough to realize that he had certainly not won the war.

Two footmen – the only two Devon had seen thus far at Castleton – arrived with the first course, and Devon could but hope that it tasted better than it looked.

He was sad to find out that it didn't, but at least the company was enjoyable.

It wasn't until later, after the dinner had concluded and the duchess had led her husband upstairs, that Devon finally had a chance to speak with Cassandra alone.

He knew she was trying to avoid him, walking out of the door just behind her parents, but it wasn't as though she could follow them into her father's bedroom.

Instead, she stood at the bottom of the stairs with her hand on the banister as though trying to decide what to do.

"I don't bite," he said from behind her, and she turned with a wary gaze on her face.

"Don't you now?"

"Well," he couldn't help but say with a wolfish grin, "not unless you ask me to. That meal has left me rather hungry."

She shook her head. "You are insufferable."

"Only to you. Everyone else finds me rather charming."

She walked away from him, down the hall and toward one of the small, more comfortable parlors near the back. A fire was blazing in the hearth, and she poured herself a drink before sinking into the overstuffed blue sofa in the corner of the room.

"You forgot to pour one for me," he noted.

She eyed him over her glass. "I do not recall inviting you in with me."

"Cassandra," he said, pouring his own glass and taking a seat on the opposite end of the sofa from her. He couldn't help but note – as he always did – just how beautiful she looked. Her auburn hair was pulled back away from her face, but not too harshly as some women wore it. It shone slightly red in the firelight, which also danced across her cheeks, highlighting her magnificent cheekbones and the soft skin he could still remember beneath his fingertips. When she lifted her drink to her plush, rosy lips, he wished that he was upon them again.

But at the moment, he was fortunate if he could get a kind word out of her, let alone a kiss.

"You were saying?" she said, raising her eyebrows, and he realized that he had become so caught up he had completely stopped speaking.

"Only that this must end."

"Your time here?" she asked, and he growled slightly at the glimmer of hope that filled her eyes.

"No. This animosity between us. Forgive me, but I fail to understand just why you hate me so. I know we should not have done what we did, but you were just as willing as I was – if not more."

She crossed her arms over her chest, and he couldn't help a quick smile, for the fact that she didn't refute him told him that he was right.

"Afterward, I offered to marry you. Consequence or not,"

he continued. "But you refused to see me, doing no more than sending a note stating all was well and there was nothing for me to be concerned about. What else should I have done, Cassandra? Where did I go wrong?"

Her eyes fell to rest on her drink, and all he could see was her face in profile, her long lashes hovering over her eyes. He wished she would share something of what she was feeling, let him in so that he wasn't in the dark about what had her so overcome.

When she didn't say anything, he found himself filling the silence. "What can I do to make things right?"

She fixed her gaze upon him. "There is nothing you can do."

"Why have you not married?" he pressed. "What are you waiting for?"

"I am ruined," she said simply. "What am I supposed to do?"

"You could still marry me," he threw out, his heart leaping into his throat, but she answered before the panic could truly set in.

"No."

"Then if not me, why not another? Only you and I know the full truth."

She was silent for a moment, her eyes fixed upon a place across the room. Then, "I told Madeline."

Devon's mouth dropped open. "Why?"

"I had to tell someone. I had far too much to talk about."

"And she shared that information?"

"No. She would never."

"Then what has you so concerned?" he asked, wondering just how he was supposed to break through and learn this woman's secrets.

"My mother and Gideon... know I am ruined. But they do not know it was you."

Devon was speechless. "How—"

"After you left that night, my mother came into the room very shortly afterward. She found me still in… disarray."

"Would that not cause her to find you a husband as soon as possible?" he asked, even as his heart ached that he had left Cassandra to face whatever came afterward herself. He had never meant it to happen, had assumed that he would do her more harm by staying, that she could claim she was alone in the room. He hadn't considered her disarray.

"She did not know the specifics, and I did not provide them. I told her that there was nothing she should be concerned about, and she believed me, thankfully. Only…"

"Only what?"

She lifted her head to look at him now, the full blaze of her blue eyes boring into him. "She questioned the morality of my behaviour. Had me sent to a hospital to mend my ways, as I'm sure you know. My family told everyone I was staying with my aunt in Bath."

He sat stiffly in his seat, staring at her. "I-I didn't know, actually. I made it a point not to ask about you, was afraid that if I did or showed any preference for you, Gideon would guess that I had intentions toward you, and you had made it very clear just how much you would abhor being with me. I never met with Gideon at the house – purposely – and never said anything about it."

She held herself stiffly, away from him, looking down at her hands. "I believe he has always felt rather guilty that I had to go away."

"Was it… was it horrible?"

"Yes," she said. "Yes, it was. I do know it could have been worse. It was run by nuns who were, at least, kind. When I returned… it seemed word had gotten out as to where I had been. No one knew anything for certain, but there was spec- ulation. So now, all of the offers I receive – for I am still the

52

daughter of a duke – are from those who want something from me other than simply my beauty or poise, or, heaven forbid, the person I am inside."

"I see," he said, looking down at his drink, which he no longer had any taste for as his stomach churned at her explanation. "I am sorry, Cassandra. If I had known—"

"*If* you had known," she repeated, shooting him a glare. "But you didn't. Because you didn't stay. You left, before I had nearly even realized what had happened between us. You were so afraid of Gideon finding out, of him feeling that you betrayed him. Well, guess what? I was the one who was left feeling betrayed. But I kept your secret, this entire time, allowing you to live life as you chose, while everything changed for me."

Devon felt like she had punched him right in the stomach, stealing all of his breath. He had to close his eyes for a moment, recover, and remind himself that he had done nothing wrong purposefully. That he hadn't known any of this, and if he had, everything would have been different.

"I am here now, Cassandra. Here for you. Looking out for you. What do you want to do?"

She looked down again, offering him a view of her beautiful profile.

"I suppose all we can do is continue on as though we are the people we were before... before that time together. I will try to be more amiable toward you, truly I will. As long as you promise to play no pranks, to make no fun, and to help in this endeavor. Because it matters – to me and to Gideon. And I know how close you and my brother are."

He nodded. She was right about that. And he would give his all to this – but not for the reason she thought. True, it was partially for Gideon, but even more so – it was for her. And it always would be her.

No matter what she thought otherwise.

CHAPTER 7

*C*assandra had held such animosity against Devon for so long that it was strange to even think of letting it go.

She knew she would never forget what had happened between them, nor what had followed, and yet... a very unsettling thought was beginning to take root in her mind. One that she had sought to deny, but after her promise of trying to forgive Devon, she knew that her feelings toward him had not all been born from what they had done together, or the pranks he had played, or the fact he had left her so quickly afterward.

No, they stemmed from the fact that she still longed for him, still yearned for him, that every time she looked at him, she nearly forgot why she had sworn him off and instead wanted him on her, with her, near her, to feel his body against hers again.

And that was half the reason she worked so hard to avoid him.

But it was not as though she had much choice in the coming weeks, so she best do all she could to live with him.

At the very least, she knew of his intelligence, that his brain worked in ways that others did not. If there was anyone outside of the family who could help with this quest, it was Devon – which was likely the very reason her brother had sought his help. That, and the fact that Gideon didn't trust many people. Outside of the family, Devon was one of the few on the very, very short list.

It was, for the foreseeable future, the two of them here at the estate – outside of her parents and the servants, of course – so she resolved that she would do as he asked and set aside her resentment of him.

Even if there was far more that she was ignoring.

"Good morning, Lord Covington," she said when she found him at the breakfast table.

"You do know Devon is fine," he said, pausing from eating his eggs and toast.

She looked around the room, taking in the lone footman who stood against the wall and the one maid who came to refill the tray.

"Lord Covington," she reiterated, and he shrugged his shoulders.

"As you wish," he said, though he couldn't help but add, "Cassandra."

Her cheeks burned and she looked from one side to the other to judge the reactions of the servants, but they were well trained and did not slip.

She swallowed hard.

"I thought that this morning we could take a turn about the gardens," he said with what he hoped was a meaningful look toward her.

"Do you truly think so?" she asked, wrinkling her nose, then leaning in as she lowered her voice so that her next words wouldn't be overheard. "I had thought perhaps the riddle was more likely to point toward the servants' quarters.

Although we would obviously need some cooperation if we wanted to find our way to search in there."

"Gideon thought the gardens for certain."

She tapped her chin. "He likely thought that because when he mentioned it to my father, that was his own first inkling upon listening to the riddle. I can see how he might consider it to be within one of the statues or ornamental pieces. But I am not so sure. There is also a collection of Greek statues upstairs in the long gallery. No one ever goes in there. It would be an obvious hiding place if it were often used, but the statues have been covered in sheets for years. They could be the people referenced in the riddle."

"Sometimes the most obvious place is the first that should be considered," Devon said, and she nodded slowly.

"You are likely right."

"Shall I meet you there an hour after we finish here?"

She nodded, even as her heart began to hammer harder in her chest at the thought of being alone with him in close quarters, although why, she wasn't entirely certain. She didn't have long to consider it, however, as before she could comment any further, her mother entered the breakfast room, putting an end to their conversation regarding the treasure.

There would be far more time for that later – which was fine. As long as the conversation concentrated on the riddle and not their past, Cassandra was happy.

For the past could stay exactly where it was.

* * *

FORTUNATELY, Cassandra's mother was not overly concerned about her whereabouts when they were here in the country. In London, she was far more cautious about where Cassandra went and with whom, for Cassandra had never completely regained her mother's trust, even after she had returned from the institution.

But here, at their country house near Colchester, Cassandra knew that her mother saw no threats, distractions, or young men who could so catch her attention.

The irony that it provided her opportunity to spend time alone with Devon was not lost on Cassandra, but then, her mother had always considered Devon like a member of the family.

Cassandra was the first to arrive in the long hall which she and Gideon had always referred to as the Greek room in their youth. One of their ancestors – which, she had no idea – had been fascinated by Greek mythology. It was, in fact, how she had come by her name, which had belonged to one of her great-great-grandmothers, if she was not mistaken. One of these statues was actually of a Cassandra, although she had no idea which one. Perhaps they would come across it in their search.

She lifted a sheet off one of the statues, producing a huge cloud of dust. She was coughing into it, waving a hand in front of her face, when the door opened and Devon walked in.

"Need a hand?" he called from across the room, and she opened her mouth to immediately refute him, but caught herself in time. He was here to help, and she had agreed to not only forgive him but to allow him to help her in this search.

"Yes, thank you," she said instead. "Some of these statues are rather tall, and I don't know how we can prevent these dust clouds in the air."

He walked at a leisurely pace toward her, and Cassandra desperately wished that he wasn't as handsome as he was, that every sight of him didn't remind her of the time they had been together. She cursed her fickle body for the way she seemed to ache for him whenever he neared – an ache that she reminded herself was temporary, whereas the pain in her heart once he moved on would be much longer lasting.

He lifted off another cover, and stared at the statue in the billowing dust that was highlighted by the sunbeams that shone through the skylights above.

"There is one consideration that we never made," he said with a look toward her. "What if the treasure is *inside* one of these statues?"

"That would be ridiculous," she countered. "These statues, while not the highest of quality, are as a whole, worthy treasures in and of themselves. We could never break them."

"Unless one of them is not as valuable as the others but was hidden here to make it appear so."

She lifted her brows. It was actually a rather intriguing supposition.

"I never thought of that."

"Which is exactly why I am here," he said with that grin she hated because of how much she loved it, one she wished he wouldn't use on her. "Is there any way to verify them?"

"I suppose we shall have to ask Gideon when he returns," she said. "He would likely know better than anyone."

Devon nodded, though he was frowning slightly. "Which brings me to my next question. Why, if the estate is in rather trying times, would Gideon not sell off some of these statues or the artwork upon the walls? Any of it would fetch a great deal."

"Yes, but what would that say about our family if we began to sell off all our belongings, that have been collected by our ancestors for centuries? He and Mother would like to retain our reputation. There are already enough reasons for people to talk, between Father and my own past."

"Our past."

She jerked her head up at him at that comment. "No one knows of your part in it."

"I do."

"Very well. *Our* past. If it became well known that we could no longer afford to keep our art collections? Mother would be beside herself. Although Gideon has said that if it comes to it, he knows what's here. I'm sure he has a detailed list of all of the items somewhere."

"He is rather organized," Devon said with a half-grin.

"That is something of an understatement."

"Well, I would suggest, then, we start by looking through all of the statues ourselves. We can make our own list and compare it to his."

"Very well," she said.

"What's this, now?" he asked, raising an eyebrow. "Is Cassandra Sutcliffe actually agreeing with me?"

"The impossible does occur now and again," she said, moving away from him before this exchange became overly friendly. They worked in companionable silence for a while, each of them moving from one side to the other until they met in the middle. The room was awash with covers all over the floor, the statues staring at them mockingly as though daring them to try to discover the secrets they held.

Cassandra looked back at them with hands on her hips. "I wish they could share with us all that they have seen and hidden over the years," she said to Devon, who was coming up behind her.

"Perhaps they will, in their own way," he said. "I'll go find paper and pen, and then I can read you each of the statue names for you to record, if you'd like."

She nodded. "That will work."

He returned shortly, catching her looking closely at the inscriptions in each statue. Most were written in Greek, but perhaps he could help identify each.

"Here you are," he said, passing her the paper and pen. "I'll begin on this side."

She was about to walk away when he reached out and caught her arm in his hand. "One moment." He lifted a hand to her face, and Cassandra's breath caught in her throat. What was he going to— he swiped his thumb over her forehead. "You had some dust," he said, his voice slightly harsh. "Gone."

"Th-thank you," she said, looking up at him. His face was just inches from hers, and she couldn't seem to move away. She was caught by the intensity of his dark gaze, his brown eyes exploring hers as though by doing so he could read all of her thoughts.

She couldn't help but drop her stare to his lips. Would it do any harm if they were to share this moment, with one more kiss? It could mean nothing, and, if she remembered correctly – how could she not – he was a most excellent kisser. She parted her lips, her tongue darting out and licking them as she waited for his face to descend.

But instead, he released her abruptly and backed away so quickly that he bumped into a statue behind him. It tottered, and he whirled around, catching it just before it went crashing to the ground.

"That was close," Cassandra said dryly, both of them aware she was referring to more than just the statue.

"I have quick hands," he said, and she just nodded as she turned away, with an "mm hmm," before she walked over to sit in one of the chairs that lined the walls. It was slightly dusty itself, and she wondered if anyone ever came in to clean this room. She supposed with the lack of servants, it made sense that they would ignore a room that was so seldom used.

Devon had thoughtfully brought her a book to set the

paper upon, and Cassandra couldn't help the laugh that emerged when she saw just which book it was.

"*An Enquiry Into the Duties of the Female Sex.*"

"Yes," he said. "Since you are apparently so familiar with this one, it seemed rather appropriate."

"I hate to ask how long it took you to search for this."

"Not overly long, actually," he said, laughter in his voice. "It was sitting out on the library table. Your mother must have left it for you."

"Of course she did," Cassandra said, sobering somewhat. She loved her mother, truly she did, but she wished that she didn't have such doubt in her. "One indiscretion, and I am forever considered disobedient."

"You do drink brandy and read romance novels of which your mother would never approve," he unhelpfully pointed out, and Cassandra lifted her chin.

"So do my friends."

"Then perhaps it is the company you keep that should be in question."

"Actually, my mother was quite pleased when I made friends with Hope and Faith Newfield, daughters of the esteemed Lord Embury."

"If only she knew."

"If only," she agreed. "Now, on to the task at hand."

He nodded. "Yes, Captain," to which she rolled her eyes, and he began to read her the names of each statue.

"You can read Greek?" she asked, although it made sense, for she knew that Gideon could, and it seemed whatever Gideon could do, so could Devon.

"I can," he confirmed. "Not as well as your brother, but I have enough knowledge to get by. We learned it at Eton."

"I see," she said. "My tutor did not teach us Greek. I wish she had. It would have been a far more useful skill than those which we did learn."

"I can imagine," he said.

They continued on the list of statues, until she had written the names out.

"I'm not seeing anything out of the ordinary," he said. "As I've been inspecting each statue, I've looked it over every which way, trying to see if there is anything of note, any secret compartments or holes or anything that might suggest the statue doesn't belong, but it seems there is nothing suspicious here."

"Very well," she said with a sigh. "Perhaps the search in this gallery was for nothing."

"Sometimes to find what one is looking for, one must rule out what is not necessary," Devon said, and she raised a brow at him.

"You have become quite the philosopher in your old age."

"Yes, as I am so much your senior."

She shook her head but couldn't help her smile as she stood, placing the paper and pen on the chair behind her. "We best clean up this mess before we depart, lest we give my mother any ideas of what we are doing."

"You don't want her to know?"

"No," she said. "The promise of treasure would either raise her hopes for them only to be dashed, or she would have the entire staff searching aimlessly and we would never find anything. Best to leave the secret as it is for now."

"And keep the search between us," he said, reaching out and taking a sheet from her. They locked eyes and she nodded slowly, even as she felt her body growing heavy at his gaze.

"Between us," she repeated, her voice just above a whisper, and she had to turn away before she was denied again.

Damn Devon Addison. The more time she spent with him, the harder it was to resist him. And that could never do. For allowing him in would only lead to one thing – trouble.

CHAPTER 8

⚜

*D*evon slept fitfully that night, tossing in the strange bed. But it wasn't the bed that was causing his sleeplessness. No, it was something – someone – else entirely. Lady Cassandra.

If he didn't know any better, he would think she was a witch who had cast a spell upon him. Every time he was around her, he could hardly keep his mind straight. All he wanted to do was wrap his arms around her, lace his fingers into her gorgeous, lush strands of auburn hair, push her against the wall, and take her again.

He groaned aloud as one hand came, unbidden, to the growing erection between his legs at the thought of her. He couldn't have her again – she had made it abundantly clear she would never marry him and he wouldn't make the same mistake twice – but he would always have the memory of her, the one that he treated himself to time and again.

Devon kept his eyes closed as he recalled their coming together. There had been a house party at the Sutcliffes' London residence, and he had been trying to convince Gideon to have a few extra drinks to loosen up, of course doing so himself to help encourage his friend. It was before his father had passed, before he had become Earl and accepted all of the responsibilities that accompanied such a role.

He suspected Cassandra had stolen a couple of the favored glasses of brandy from her brother, but she had been well within her right mind – he would never take a woman who was not aware of her actions, that was for certain. Especially Cassandra.

Still, they had likely each been less inhibited than they would have otherwise been, and he had actually been looking for Gideon when Devon had found her in the library instead. He had asked what she was doing, and she told him she was trying to find facts about the badger's eating habits of all things in order to win a friendly bet she had made with Lord Ferrington.

She had been suspicious of Devon's motivation when he had asked her more about the topic, convinced that he was just out to trick her, make fun of her, or to try to prove her wrong in some way.

"Are you part of some prank on me, my lord? Or are you working alongside Lord Ferrington?" she had asked, to which he had shaken his head before placing a finger on her lips.

"Not at all," he had responded. "In fact, I am intrigued by *you*, Lady Cassandra."

"I thought I was your friend's little sister, good only to prank and make a fool of."

"Not anymore," he had responded, not interested in speaking of it further, instead asking her more questions about this bet and the badger. Apparently the fact in question was as to whether the badger was a carnivore. He could tell she had been wary at first, but eventually she had shown him what she found in a book, responding to him treating her like an equal and not a little girl to be tortured by pranks, as he had always done before.

The truth was, he had always been affected by her in one way or another, but when he was a younger man, he hadn't had any idea what he was supposed to do about those emotions, so he'd shown his interest by teasing her and convincing her brother to play jokes on her. Any reaction from her, as annoyed as she usually was, was better than her completely ignoring him.

That night, however, was different. It had been just the two of them, and he had shown rapt attention in her without any games or tricks.

They had been sitting there on the sofa together when she had turned to look at him, her face tilting to the right in that most becoming way of hers. He had been so lost in her that he hadn't had time to consider his own emotions, nor the ramifications of the two of them enjoying more from one another than simply conversation.

He moaned aloud in the present, remembering the sweet softness of her lips, the way she had opened up to him, with complete trust, giving her all to him, even though she would have been well aware that she shouldn't have.

Devon had never meant for it to go any further than that. He had thought they would kiss, then go their separate ways and either never speak of it again, or perhaps he would continue to court her and show her that he could be the man for her, that she was more to him than simply Gideon's sister.

If he went about it properly, he was sure that his friend would accept his courtship of his sister. For who would be better to marry her than the man Gideon considered closer than any other in the world?

Then all had changed when Cassandra had pushed her breasts against him, and he had figured that one caress couldn't hurt. They had been so full in his hands, filling them perfectly, and soon feeling them through the fabric of her gown hadn't been enough. He had slipped his hand inside, had been lost in the perfection of them.

And oh, how she had responded. She had thrown her head back, baring her neck to him, and he had taken full advantage, kissing his way down her soft skin. When she had pressed her hand against the bulge in his trousers, he had nearly exploded right there within himself, but had managed to take hold of his control even as she had slipped her hand beneath his waistband.

He had stopped then, had managed to tell her that they shouldn't be doing this, but all she had done was whisper, "I know," before she had continued her exploration and he became a man lost to her.

When his hands had slipped up her skirts, he had meant to do no more than use his fingers upon her, to bring her pleasure he doubted she'd ever found before – although this was Cassandra, so one could never be completely certain – but then she was begging for more, he was caught in his own need for release, and with one quick question as to whether she was sure, he was seated within her – and so fully home that he had nearly lost control and allowed a tear to fall from his eye.

He had moved inside of her, finding a rhythm, a dance that was meant for the two of them alone. He knew that nothing would ever compare to the feeling of Cassandra around him, in front of him, in his hands, him within her. The feeling of her was indelibly imprinted in his memory, and thank goodness it was so. He'd had enough sense to finish – after she did – within his handkerchief instead of inside of her, although he had known that nothing was for certain.

Afterward, they had stood there staring at one another in

shock, both of them breathing heavily, dishevelled, and uncertain about what it all meant.

That was when they had heard a noise from outside the room – of course they had, there had been an ongoing party in the house – and Devon had decided that his best course of action was to leave. He would marry Cassandra, he had told himself – what other choice did he have, not that he was completely against the idea – but not like this. Not in a compromising position, which would break all of the trust between both him and Cassandra, and him and Gideon, the person who was closest to him in the world.

He would court her properly, he had decided.

But he had made one mistake.

He hadn't actually shared that information with her in the moment.

Instead, he had murmured a quick, "that could be Gideon," as he had hastily fastened his trousers.

Then with a nod to her, his usual charm escaping him, he had fled through the door across the room before the two of them could be found together in such disarray.

He had never stopped to consider what it would mean when she was caught – alone.

Which made him a fool and her hatred of him rather justified.

When she had avoided him afterward, refusing to see him or speak to him, he had thought that she hadn't been interested in his affections, but had used him for the experience. He had never guessed the truth of what she had been going through.

The thought of it all and what she'd had to withstand now had him unable to finish what he had started. Instead, he lay there, panting, staring up at the ceiling, wondering just what he had done – and how he was going to fix it.

He had wanted so badly to kiss her in the long gallery. If

he hadn't been mistaken, she was ready, open to it, would have kissed him back. But, knowing her, that would only have made her push him away once more afterward. No, it was better that he did this the right way. Before he fulfilled the longing they had for one another, he must show her that she could trust him, that she could like him as a person.

Even if it was going to be immeasurably more work.

* * *

As much as Devon had been a great help yesterday in searching the long gallery, Cassandra decided that after their near-kiss, she would be best exploring the gardens alone. For her family still maintained a gardener on staff, and while some of the grounds had fallen into disarray, the gardens themselves immediately in front of Castleton were beautiful; rather romantic, one would say. She could hardly imagine the trouble she and Devon might find if they were to search them together.

The problem, she realized once she began her search, was that she had no idea just exactly what she was looking for.

She ran her hands over the statues she came across, trying to find crevices or hiding places within them or any of the pieces that would have been permanent. Obviously, all of the flower beds and hedges couldn't have held anything – they were too often reviewed by the gardener, and nothing would have lasted overly long when out in the elements.

She had her elbows resting on the edge of the fountain, as she bent over and peered within, trying to determine whether there could be anything hiding behind the stones beneath the depths, when a figure appeared beside her, causing her to shriek in surprise and nearly topple over, until a warm hand reached out and caught her.

"Devon, you scared me!" she exclaimed, bringing a hand

to her breast. "Why would you sneak up on me like that?"

"Perhaps the better question is why would you sneak away from me when we were to search together?" he asked, slowly sliding his hand away from her and crossing his arms over his chest. "Was this not to be a joint search?"

"I thought perhaps it best that I do it alone today," she said with a shrug as though it didn't mean anything, but he narrowed his eyes at her as a bird's call sliced through the silence.

"You're scared," he said, and she leaned back away from him at that, trying not to notice how handsome he looked, as he lifted a hand to hold onto his hat when the breeze began to pick up.

"Pardon me?"

"I said that you are scared," he repeated, fixing his tall, straight hat more securely to his head. "After what happened in the long gallery, you are afraid of being close to me, of what could happen if we are alone together once more."

"Nothing happened in the long gallery," she said, holding her chin high, reminding herself that it was the truth – nothing *had* happened, although only because Devon hadn't allowed it to. She would have done whatever he would have liked in the moment. Which was exactly the problem. She was currently in the predicament of having to trust Devon more than herself, which was not exactly the most ideal situation.

"Right," he said with a grin. "If that is what you would like to believe."

She would have *liked* to have told him exactly what she thought of that comment, but at the moment, she thought perhaps it was best to continue on her current conviction and ignore that there had been any moment between them – it would give him too much satisfaction if she were to admit it.

Although she couldn't help but wonder just why he had denied her. Did he not feel *anything* toward her? Yes, she hated that she wanted him with as fierce of a passion as she had the night they had come together, but want him she did. Did he have no desire for her? Had it all fled over the years and did his affection now rest with another – or, perhaps, anyone *but* her?

For that would hurt far worse than she would have liked.

Sometimes she wondered about other women he had been with – who had come before, who had come after, how they compared to her. But she knew that she should have no say in it, no opinion. She had been the one who had chosen not to speak with him again.

But all that was in the past, she reminded herself. She was here now, present. And she needed to accept what was and not what could have been.

"How long have you been searching?" he asked her now, apparently moving on himself, back to the present moment and matters beyond the two of them.

"Perhaps an hour," she said before finally deciding that, at this point, she should welcome any ideas he had. "The truth is, I'm not entirely sure where to search. I tried looking through all of the garden statues, all of the small edifices and any permanent fixtures, but I cannot find anything. I wish I better understood the clue."

"Don't we all," he said dryly, before reaching out a hand toward her. "Come, let's take a walk around as we think this through."

"But—"

He bent his outstretched fingers a couple of times in invitation, and she sighed as she reached out and accepted it. "Very well," she said, although she didn't place her hand on his offered arm, instead keeping it to herself.

For she couldn't risk getting too close once more.

CHAPTER 9

*D*evon could both sense and understand
Cassandra's hesitancy. But even so, he wished that
she would trust him slightly more.

He had arrived for breakfast, surprised to find that she
had already eaten, for he hadn't known her to be an early
riser in the past. But he had shrugged it off – until he had
glimpsed her through the window in the hall, touring the
gardens by herself.

Here he thought that they had come to an understanding,
at least when it came to solving the riddle and finding the
treasure.

But when he had discovered her staring into the fountain,
he had felt both her despair as well as her wish for something
more, and he had waited a moment before disturbing her. He
could purport it was to give her time, but the truth was, he
had been appreciating her beauty, so at home here in the
green splendour of the garden, until he had made his presence known.

"So what is your grand idea?" she asked now, and he
looked down at her profile, longing to reach out and tuck the

one errant curl the wind had swept loose back behind her ear.

"You say you have searched throughout the garden."

"I have."

"I suggest that we look once more, and then broaden our quest."

She looked up at him then, her eyes instantly lighting as she quickly realized just what he was referencing.

"The ruins. Of course. How could I be such a fool to not have thought of them?"

"I would never call you a fool, Cassandra."

"No, but it makes perfect sense. Gideon missed it too. They have been there longer than anything else upon the estate and no one ever goes within them, only perhaps to walk by them. They were, at one point, where people laid their heads."

"I am just unsure if we should explore them today," he said, wishing now that he had searched them himself first.

"Why ever not?"

"How are we to know if they are safe?" he asked. "No one has likely walked among them for years. I know Gideon and I used to explore them as children, and I recall there being loose rock and pieces of the ruins apt to fall around us. We are lucky we didn't get ourselves killed at the time. If I were to take you there and something were to happen to you, Gideon would never forgive me."

She fixed him with a look, and he instantly realized that he had made two mistakes – the first, to suggest that he would just be upset because of Gideon's reaction, the second in placing a challenge before her.

"I can assure you that I am equally adept at handling my footing as you would be," she said. "In fact, I would wager I am even more so based on all of the training I had to go through over the years on the proper way to walk, to dance, to carry myself."

"I never suggested that you wouldn't have the ability," he said, trying to take back the words. "Only that, perhaps, I should make sure all is safe first."

"We go now," she said decisively, and he looked down, ensuring, at least, that she was wearing appropriate boots. "If anything should happen, I shall take full responsibility," she added.

"That is hardly comforting."

They were, however, already walking toward the ruins, and Devon knew that he had no choice now. He was all too aware that once Cassandra made up her mind about something, there was no stopping her.

"Very well," he said, accepting his defeat, as they walked away from the grounds toward where the terrain became less manicured, where nature had been allowed to return. There was still a worn path through the trees, one that was more often used by horses – most likely the duke's, for he still ventured out of doors along with Anderson, as far as Devon was aware – but it was not completely ideal for walking, and Devon kept a close eye on Cassandra, although it seemed that she had been correct and was able to navigate the terrain as well as he.

"You know I used to follow you out here," she finally said after some silence, and he turned to her with surprise.

"You did?"

"I did," she said with a nod, a reflective smile crossing her face. "I was so bored with the needlepoint and lessons that Mother tried to force upon me. Instead, I would sneak out and follow you and Gideon. You had such fun out here, playing hide and seek and pretending that you were living among the ruins. I envied you."

"Why didn't you tell us that you were there?" he asked. "You could have joined us."

"You would never have allowed it," she scoffed. "I'm sure you would have played some elaborate trick on me had you known. In fact, do you remember the time I became lost, when Mother and Father couldn't find me?"

Devon did, in fact. His family had been visiting, as they often did in the summer months, and he recalled her parents becoming distraught when the governess had alerted them that Cassandra was nowhere to be found. He and Gideon had been blamed at first, until they made it clear that they had been out playing and had no idea to where Cassandra could have gone.

One of the grooms had finally found her, out of doors as she had returned soaked from the rain that had begun while she had been out, but he hadn't known where she had been.

"You were in the ruins that entire time?" he asked.

"I was," she nodded. "I had followed you, but you had nearly caught me, so I hid and my foot became wedged in a crack behind some broken wall. My foot was stuck, and I couldn't get it out. I tried everything. I wondered if anyone was ever going to find me. Then the rain began, and I became certain that was where everything would end for me." She paused for a moment. "I still don't like thunderstorms."

"I can imagine," he said, additional guilt beginning to creep in. "I'm sorry."

She laughed wryly. "*This* circumstance was not your fault at all," she said. "It was my own. I allowed my pride to get in the way. When I saw you and Gideon leave, I was stuck. I could have called out to you for help, but I didn't want you to know what I had done. I could have saved myself a lot of trouble and fear. I was lucky I was found."

"That you were," he said, but the truth was, so was he. He

couldn't imagine his world without Cassandra in it. "Have you returned to the ruins since?"

"I've walked or ridden by them a few times," she mused as they stopped in front of the ruins, looking up at them. "But I've never had reason to go within."

"I never thought to ask Gideon just what these ruins used to be," he said. "Do you know?"

"I believe this was once the main house," she said. "But that must have been at least a couple of hundred years ago. I'm sure if something was hidden here, the building would have already been in ruin."

"Well, then, it should be much easier to find." He held his hand out to her. "Shall we?"

She eyed it as though it was uncertain food of a questionable age but, not being a woman to back down from a challenge, determination crossed her face as she reached up and wrapped her fingers around his.

Lightning raced from where their bare skin touched, up his arms to the very core of his body.

This woman made him feel things that he never had before and he never would again with any other, that was for certain.

He saw the shock in her own eyes, and knew that if he wanted this moment with her, he could have it, but decided that he would continue on with their initial quest instead. He kept her hand firmly within his as they began to navigate their way up the path on its slight incline, his eyes open for any sign of impediment on the path or within the ruins themselves.

"If something is hidden, it could be anywhere," he said, lifting a hand to shade his eyes as he looked around, remembering the various nuances of the remnants of the building around them.

"We must be thorough, then," she said. "We'll begin at one

side and work our way to the other. Do you want to start on one end and I will start on the other?"

"No." He shook his head, his jaw set. "We shall search together."

"But we shall be faster—"

"No," he repeated, more firmly this time. He was not about to leave her alone. "Together."

She must have realized that there was no use in arguing with him, that this was one of the few things he was not going to relent upon, for she reluctantly nodded, agreeing with him.

Fortunately, it was the right time of day and the light was agreeable to where they were searching, although it was beginning to fade and Devon had to wonder if it was due to the time of day or if it was simply clouding over.

Many of the ruin walls still held their original shape, so it was easy enough to each take a dilapidated section and search among its crevices for any signs of blemish or cracks where something could have been hidden.

They often had to dislodge plants or other vegetation, and now and then Devon would reach out to remove an odd brick from the path in front of Cassandra.

"If you paid the same attention to where we were searching as you did to the ground around us, then we might be having much better luck," she couldn't help but murmur, and his head snapped up at that.

"I apologize for seeing to your safety," he said, not masking his sarcasm. "But as it is, we should be getting back soon. You must be getting hungry if you were already outside an hour before I was."

"I'm fine."

"But—"

"I said that I am fine," she said firmly. "You must believe me."

"Very well," he said as they left their current area toward the back of the ruins, which would have been the rear of the building — castle or manor house at one point in time. "One more row and then that will be it for the day."

"If that is what we *both* decide."

"Cassandra," he exhaled with a sigh as they stepped into the new territory. As he looked over at her, however, he took his eyes off the ground around them, and he was the one whose toe hit a brick in front of them. He stumbled, attempted to catch himself, and then went falling forward, reaching out a hand to the remnants of the brick wall before him.

He surprised himself when he caught the wall, but, unfortunately, he must have been far too much weight for its current uncertain state to hold and he soon found that despite his initial stop, he was continuing to fall forward even lower – as he had broken the wall and it was crashing around them.

"Devon!" he heard Cassandra call out, but he was willing her away, hoping she would stay back from any of the bricks that could hit her.

She, however, did not seem to be listening to his silent command as she continued forward, one of her hands reaching out to grip his jacket as she attempted to either catch him or pull him backward.

Which ended with them both lying in a heap on the ground, her body slightly covering his as bricks littered the dirt around them.

Devon could only groan as he lay on his back, arms spread out wide – with Cassandra splayed over top of him.

He reached out, his hands running over her face.

"Cassandra, are you all right? I'm so sorry, I shouldn't have—"

"I'm completely fine," she said, her fingers digging into his chest as she started to push herself up. "What about *you?* You're the one who fell, who knocked down this entire wall after telling me that it was very possible I would hurt myself. Sometimes you must listen to your own advice."

"I know." He winced as something sharp – likely a stone or piece of brick – cut into his back. Cassandra caught the pain on his face and narrowed her eyes as she ran them over him, inspecting him.

"What's wrong?"

"Nothing."

But it wasn't so much the ache that was bothering him – it was Cassandra's body on top of his. It seemed that her touch was enough to cut through any pain that might be otherwise affecting him.

"Are you *sure* you are fine?" she asked, and he nodded, looking up into her face.

"Why, Cassandra, is that genuine concern for me that I see on your face?"

"Well, of course," she said, quickly masking her emotion. "I could never allow anything to happen to you. Gideon would never forgive me. It was why I pushed you out of the way."

"I was trying to keep *you* out of the way!" he exclaimed. "I am the one that should be taking care of you."

"Why?" she challenged him. "Because you are a man?"

"Well…" He knew this wasn't going to be the right answer, but he wasn't sure what else to say. "Yes."

"That's ridiculous."

"How so?" he countered. "Even if that wasn't the norm, Gideon asked me to look after you."

"And I am telling you that I can look after myself," she said. "It is not always about what Gideon wants."

She pushed herself up off him now, but he reached up and caught her around the upper arms.

"It's not just what Gideon asked," he said roughly. "I cannot allow anything to happen to you."

"Because Gideon would never speak to you again?" she said somewhat mockingly, but he ignored her tone as he shook his head.

"No," he said roughly. "Because *I* would be destroyed if anything ever did."

And at that declaration, he did what he had been wanting to do since he had walked into the parlor but a few weeks ago, what he knew he still shouldn't do yet he couldn't prevent himself from following through with any longer.

He leaned up and took her lips with his.

She stilled for a moment, and he wondered if she was going to pull back away from him. Knowing her, he was just as likely to end up with a slap to the face as he was with her affections. But he waited patiently, and after but another moment he was rewarded.

For not only did she allow him to kiss her, but she kissed him back with as much ferocity as she put into anything. She allowed her weight to fall down upon him as she held herself up with her elbows framing his head around his ears. Devon had wondered if her desire for him was anything like his was for her, but if this kiss was any indication, it was equally matched.

She drank him in as if she had been parched for him, and he gave back as well as he could from his prone position on the ground. Part of him wished that he was above her, that he could be the one to drive this kiss, but he was also enjoying her attack.

For no matter what she said, she could no longer deny that she was affected by him.

CHAPTER 10

*C*assandra knew that if there was anything in this world she should not be doing, it was kissing Devon Addison. Lord Covington. The man who had tormented her through childhood, who had been her first kiss, her first everything, who had then left her to face a myriad of consequences while he had continued on with his very privileged life until he had inherited his title.

Yet she had enjoyed his company over the last couple of days, and, despite all of her efforts otherwise, had never rid herself of her wish to see him again, to be with him again, to know him again in more ways than she already did.

Then his lips had touched hers and she lost every bit of rational thought she still possessed.

She knew she should stop, that this was how she had gotten herself into trouble before – by allowing her desire for him to take over everything else. But she seemed to be addicted to the feel of his lips under hers, the softness of his hair around her fingers, the groans of pleasure he made as she kissed him back.

She felt as though her body was made for his, and she

wanted to take all that she could from him, and, interestingly enough, give what she could in turn.

Cassandra had no idea what would have happened had the loud crack of thunder not cut through the sky. She had nearly forgotten her surroundings, and she flinched so hard she was sure she had likely hurt him once more, but instead of jumping off him, she found herself gripping him even tighter.

"Is there a storm?" she asked, hearing the raggedness of her breathing, pretending to herself it was due to her fear but knowing it was for another reason entirely.

"Must be," he said, and she was glad to see that he, at least, also seemed somewhat shaken by their kiss. Or maybe he had hit his head as he had fallen – she couldn't be completely sure. "We should be getting back."

"We should," she said, and it was only then she realized that she was still lying completely flat on top of him, her breasts pressed against his chest, as a certain protrusion was digging into her stomach.

She gasped when she realized just what it was and she scrambled back off him, although perhaps a little too quickly as he let out an "oof" when her elbow landed soundly in his stomach.

"Sorry," she muttered before she got to her feet, holding out a hand to help him up. He eyed her with a quirk of his brow before he did take her hand but pushed himself to standing without actually giving her any of his weight.

He didn't let go once he came to his feet, and it was then that the first raindrop fell, landing on Cassandra's nose and then rolling right off it to the ground.

"We better hurry," he said, tugging at her hand and pulling her along with him. They kept a good pace as they hurried down the hill, mindful of their footing on the wet surface as they went. Cassandra had to take quick steps to keep up with

Devon's long legs, but she was as motivated as he once the raindrops fell faster. She was wearing a morning gown, one which allowed for some fluidity of movement, but of course she had nothing like the freedom provided by the breeches Devon wore.

Cassandra truly wouldn't have minded the rain – that never scared her – but then lightning rent the darkening clouds and the sky let out another crack of thunder. She couldn't help the cry that escaped her, and Devon turned around, pulling her in close by his side as he now ran with her held against him instead of walking behind him. Cassandra didn't want to admit how much comfort she found with his strong arm around her waist. She had always prided herself on her ability to take care of herself, no matter what came her way, but she would take what he offered in this moment – at least until they were safe within the house.

They had just reached the gardens when the rain began to come down in torrents, and they sprinted the rest of the way along the manicured paths until they reached the side of the house, climbing the slick stone steps before Devon pushed open the glass library doors, which were, thankfully, unlocked.

They stood there in the entrance, dripping wet, staring at one another in shock. Devon's eyes were intense, and as he opened his mouth, she knew exactly what he was going to ask – was she all right – but before he did, she took in his hair plastered to his head, the water dripping down his face, his soiled, expensive clothing, and she couldn't help herself.

Her lips curled up into a smile, and then she began to laugh.

Devon's mouth dropped open in incredulity as though he thought she had gone mad, but after a moment it appeared his resistance grew thin, and his own lips widened as he joined in her mirth.

Soon they were laughing together as the rain dripped off of them, and Cassandra didn't know how long they would have stayed like that had thunder not boomed again outside of the window, and she jumped – right into his arms once more.

They wrapped around her as though they had been prepared for her, and she froze as she realized just what she had done – she had gone to him for comfort.

"I'm sorry," she said, nearly tripping over her feet as she stepped backward, immediately missing his warmth.

"Nothing to be sorry for," he said, clearing his throat as his eyes wandered away from her face and down her body, and she followed his gaze – then gasped when she realized what he was staring at.

The rain had wet her dress, and the fine muslin was now plastered to her skin, the pale yellow of the fabric doing nothing to hide her nipples, which were now practically protruding through the dress. He cleared his throat as he looked away, although his cheeks had turned a shade of red at how obviously affected he was by her.

"I should—"

"You should—"

She laughed nervously as they both spoke together.

"—probably go change," she finished.

"Yes, I do not suppose your mother would be pleased to discover that you were caught out in the rain."

"I could explain it, but she would have questions."

"We probably should not have been unchaperoned."

"No, we most certainly should not have been."

Goodness, but she despised this awkwardness between them. She supposed it was a result of the simmering tension that had begun in the ruins – or the moment she had laid eyes on him once more, if she were being honest – but one way or another, she had a feeling that this had to be put to bed somehow. She just wasn't sure how they should go about doing so.

* * *

DEVON DIDN'T SEE Cassandra for the rest of the day – nor the next. He knew they should have been searching, but she had claimed a headache and remained in her room, or at least far from him. He knew the truth – that she had been as affected as he by how close they had grown the previous day, and she likely was equally unsure just what they were to do about it.

At some point, however, they would have to discuss it, and he wanted to be prepared. He wondered what she would say if he told her how he truly felt. He wasn't sure she was quite ready to put the past behind her.

All he could do for now was show her that he was not the man he had once been – and wait for Gideon to return. For once he saw Gideon again, he was going to tell him what he truly felt for his sister, and ask permission to court her properly, to do this right – if she would let him.

Cassandra finally appeared at dinner, her cheeks pale until she looked at him – and then he noted the rosy hint that appeared, telling him it was as he thought, and she was having trouble remaining close to him without remembrance of all that had happened between them – and all that could still occur if they continued on.

"Cassandra, I am so glad that you are feeling better," the duchess said once they were seated around the table. The duke was not present tonight, his valet informing them that he was not himself, which meant he was likely having an episode of some sort.

"Thank you, Mother," she said with a nod, her eyes everywhere but on Devon, as though she couldn't look at him, afraid that she would give something of herself away.

"I do have some exciting news," the duchess continued. "We received an invitation today. The Newfields are hosting a party in two days' time. They have invited us to attend."

"Would they not have just arrived in the country?" Cassandra asked, surprise on her face, which made sense as Devon knew she was close to Hope and Faith, daughters of Lord Embury

"You know Lady Embury," the duchess said. "She likes everyone to know where she is and how well they are doing. I'm sure the servants have been preparing this event for ages. She is calling it the opening of the summer season."

"Well, despite the surprise, I am looking forward to seeing Hope and Faith," Cassandra said. "While they are too far away for regular visits, at least we can have these few events."

"How far is the travel?" Devon asked, and the duchess looked at him in surprise as though she had forgotten he was there.

"A half-day's journey," she said. "We shall stay overnight and return the next day."

"Very well," Devon said, considering that it wouldn't take too much time away from their search – which had stalled as it was.

He felt Cassandra's gaze on him then and turned to look at her, but she quickly jerked her head away.

"Will you accompany us, then, Lord Covington?" the duchess asked, to which he gave a quick nod. He did usually enjoy such events, but the truth was that his interest in attending stemmed more so from the fact that he had no desire to leave Cassandra – especially when she would find herself in the company of other young men.

"Of course," he said with a wide smile, one he turned and directed at Cassandra – whether she wanted it or not. "I look forward to escorting the two of you."

"We do appreciate it," the duchess said. "It is lovely to have you around, especially with Gideon away."

There was a look on her face that told him she still wasn't entirely sure what he was doing there, but he appreciated that she hadn't asked too many questions.

Whether she'd have some when he made it clear that he was intent on having Cassandra's hand, he wasn't sure.

But until then, he would play the part.

And, he thought with some amusement as he sent a wink Cassandra's way, he would enjoy himself while he did so.

CHAPTER 11

*C*assandra knew she should have spent the past few days searching for the treasure or trying to make some sense of the riddle, but instead she had become rather engrossed in the latest novel she and her friends were reading – and, she could admit, she knew hiding away was the very best way to avoid Devon.

She had become rather adept at it over the years, although it was slightly more difficult when he was sleeping within the same house as she was. At this particular moment, however, she had no choice but to acknowledge him, trapped as they were within the carriage. Of course, having her mother within helped diffuse any tension or temptation that otherwise would surely have been present.

They spoke of everything and nothing on the journey to Newfield Manor, until about an hour away, Cassandra's mother fell asleep. Cassandra kept her eyes fixed outside the window, even as she could feel Devon's gaze upon her.

"Is your plan to simply avoid me forever?" His deep voice finally cut through her thoughts, and she turned her head sharply toward him.

"I am not avoiding you."

He lifted one of his generous brows, that intense gaze causing a quiver deep in her belly.

"Cassandra. There were two things I would never have thought you could become – a liar or a coward."

She sat up straight at that. "Excuse me! I am neither of those things."

"Except that you are certainly acting like both."

Deep within, she knew he was right. She typically met every challenge head on, unafraid to back down or show any fear. The problem with Devon was that it wasn't the man she couldn't handle – it was her own feelings toward him.

She glanced toward her mother, who appeared to be sound asleep, although Cassandra couldn't be entirely certain that she wasn't listening to their conversation.

"We shouldn't speak of this now," she whispered, which appeared to amuse Devon even further.

"Very well. When would you prefer?"

"Never," she said honestly, sighing when she saw that her answer made his smile widen. "But if we must, then once we return to Castleton."

"You will provide me a moment of your time alone, then?"

"I will," she promised, wondering as she did if she was setting herself up for another encounter with him that she should be avoiding. Although she knew, within, that as much as she tried, she would never be able to keep herself completely away from him. His pull on her was too strong. She would simply have to do her best to remain stoic until he left their estate. Eventually he would have to see to his own responsibilities, would he not?

Thankfully, he let go of the topic for the remainder of the ride, and soon enough, Cassandra's mother awoke and they arrived at their destination. Cassandra wondered how many guests would be in attendance, for Lady Embury was always quite eager to invite as many titled guests who lived within a reasonable distance as she could to her gatherings.

Devon offered both Cassandra and her mother an arm as he escorted them up the stairs, and she gratefully greeted her friends, who were waiting within along with their parents to welcome their guests.

"Oh, I am so glad to see you," she said to the sisters, who said more with their expressions than their words as they noted her arrival with Devon and without her brother. "I have much to share with you, although most will have to wait until later," she said meaningfully.

They nodded as there wouldn't be time at the present, and soon enough, Cassandra was shown to her bedroom. There would be much more time tonight to tell them all that had occurred – regarding treasure hunting. As for her encounters with Devon... that might be a topic best avoided for now.

* * *

FOR THE SECOND time in a matter of weeks, Devon found himself in a new country house, a strange bedroom, and Lady Cassandra on his mind.

The fact she was sharing each home with him was actually somewhat comforting, for at least he knew he could keep an eye on her.

The dinner and dance were to be held that evening, of course, and in the meantime, Devon went searching for the billiards room, which turned out to hold none other than Lord Whitehall, better known to the lot of them as Anthony Davenport. He wasn't the closest of his friends, for Devon had always had a difficult time understanding Whitehall's reluctance to enjoy life but rather to focus on what could go wrong. Still, Whitehall understood Devon better than most and had fit well in their small circle of men seeking out adventure, despite usually questioning ideas brought forward by anyone else.

"Whitehall, didn't expect to see you here," Devon said, clapping the man on the shoulder.

"Nor you," the viscount said. "What brings you all this way to Harwich?"

"Well," Devon said, looking around to ensure that they would not be overheard, "you recall Gideon's riddle?"

"Of course."

"I accompanied him to Castleton to help search for clues. Then Gideon was called away on some pressing matters at a secondary estate, so I am doing what I can in his absence. He should hopefully return shortly."

"You are staying at Castleton alone, then?"

"The rest of the family is there," Devon said, not mentioning Cassandra's name lest Whitehall read something into it. "And Gideon should be back soon."

"Your own family is fine with that?"

Devon hadn't heard from his brother since he had told his family that he would be delayed in meeting them at their own estate near Newmarket, but he hadn't been overly concerned. Once he was finished with this business, he would spend the rest of the summer with them. His father had always ensured that he had excellent stewards and men-of-business in place to deal with everyday matters, and his brother could deal with any urgent situations that arose. Devon hadn't had any concerns with allowing them to continue to do what they did best.

"My family spends enough time with me that I'm sure they are happy to have a reprieve," he said instead, to which Whitehall simply grunted – as was his way.

"And just how is your treasure hunt going?" Whitehall

asked.

"We haven't found anything as of yet," Devon said with a sigh. "Although I suppose you could say we have determined where the treasure *isn't* as opposed to where it is."

"I thought you said Addison was away."

"He is."

"Then who is this 'we'?"

Devon realized his mistake too late, although he supposed there wasn't much harm in sharing this part of the story.

"Before Gideon left, Lady Cassandra revealed that she also got her hands on a copy of the riddle. Apparently, its author made a draft version that was stuck in some book she was reading. An unlikely coincidence, but there you have it. She has insisted on helping with the search. It is actually part of the reason Gideon asked me to stay – to ensure she doesn't impede our hunt or get into any trouble."

"That cannot be much help, having to look out for a woman as you try to make your own discovery," Whitehall remarked dryly, to which Devon reacted with annoyance within that surprised him.

"It has actually not been as difficult as you might think. She has had some rather keen ideas," he said as mildly as he could.

"I see," Whitehall said, the last comment obviously stirring some suspicions as he murmured, "Interesting."

"Shall we try a game?" Devon asked, gesturing to the billiards table, to which Whitehall nodded, thankfully allowing himself to be distracted from their conversation, although Devon knew he was intelligent enough to realize his aim.

If only he could distract himself so easily.

Hours later, after handily defeating Lord Whitehall, Devon entered the ballroom, pausing for a moment to take in all before him.

"Lady Embury certainly outdid herself," Whitehall said from behind him, and Devon looked back, nodding.

"I'm not sure I've ever seen anything quite like this."

The entire room was decorated to resemble some celestial paradise – heaven, he supposed, or perhaps simply the clouds? Devon couldn't be certain, but he had the distinct feeling that he wasn't quite good enough to walk within the atmosphere, that he hadn't met the qualifications.

When he took a look around at some of the other guests, however, he quickly lost any concern that he wouldn't fit in, as he knew some of these gentlemen would be much more at home in a gaming hell or a brothel than they would in such a ballroom.

"Is St. Peter supposed to be waiting somewhere to let us in?" Devon asked jokingly as he noticed the harp player in a corner, dressed in a toga – perhaps this was to be the heaven of the ancient Greek gods and goddesses, then.

"It seems we are all free to enter," Whitehall said, and the two of them sought out a drink as they stood to the side and kept their eye on the door – ostensibly to see who would enter, although Devon was interested in the arrival of just one particular guest.

And there she was now. Cassandra took slow steps into the room, as though uncertain if she also belonged. Her gaze roved around until it landed somewhere to the left of him, and he wished that the genuine smile rising in her cheeks was for him. But no, he realized as he watched her, she was looking at Hope and Faith Newfield. At least it wasn't another gentleman.

"Sometimes I forget that Ashford has such a comely sister," Whitehall said, and Devon found his hands tightening, the one not holding the glass forming a fist. Whitehall was his friend, but he should have no claim over Cassandra –

although neither should Devon, at least until he spoke to Gideon.

"Yes," he said in a clipped tone before taking a sip of his brandy, wishing that he could fetch a glass for Cassandra and bring it to her, for it was one gesture he knew she would actually appreciate. But if anyone were to discover him, he would likely bring further shame to her name as well as questions regarding his own actions in trying to force alcohol on a young woman.

"There was that whole business with her indiscretions and being sent away from her family," Whitehall continued, and Devon had to wonder if everyone but him was aware of what had happened to Cassandra.

"I'm sure it was all a misunderstanding," he murmured instead. "She has always been quite... polite, as far as I am aware."

Of course, that was rather far from the truth, but what was he supposed to say? That the two had tortured one another with their words and pranks because they didn't know how else to otherwise manage the tensions between them besides making love to one another in a drawing room?

She looked especially beautiful tonight, of course, although Devon found that he was always thinking that about her. Her dress was a pale blue with a green touch to it, causing her to look like the angel she was among the white silk that had been hung upon the walls. She wore a small gold piece around her neck, the aquamarine jewel nestled between her breasts, her hair softly pulled back, allowing a few tendrils to fall around her face in ruddy brown waves.

Devon wished that he could go to her, to claim her as his own, for he saw the hungry gazes that were trained on her. But she was not his – not yet. Only in his own heart and mind.

Which he hoped to change. Starting tonight.

CHAPTER 12

"I have tried to make sense of your riddle, Cassandra, truly I have," Hope said from where the three of them stood at the edge of the ballroom, waiting for the musicians to begin playing. It was an eclectic mix of guests. There was nobility who lived close enough to make the journey in less than a day, as well as some of the local gentry, who took pride in being invited to an event held by Lord and Lady Embury. Cassandra wondered how the dancing would proceed, if any of the local gentlemen would be inclined to ask for her to join them. She rather hoped so, for it became dull to dance with the same men again and again.

She tried not to think about one certain gentleman, who she had danced with but once, before they had taken part in another kind of dance altogether.

She had noticed him when she had entered the room, although she tried not to allow him or anyone else to see just what effect his presence had upon her. He had been speaking to Lord Whitehall, who she was surprised to see, and had felt the gazes of both men. She could only wonder what Devon might have to say about her presence and the time they had recently spent together.

Of course, if she had turned to meet his stare, she would have been in good company, for it seemed that every other woman present was also keenly aware of him. How could they not, with the way his dark chestnut hair swept back from his forehead, his blue eyes crisp and haunting, his stature dominant and demanding attention?

"Cassandra?"

She jerked her gaze back toward Hope, who was staring at her with some knowing in her blue eyes. Faith didn't hide her suspicion at all.

"Has a certain Lord Covington so captured your attention?" she asked, and Cassandra straightened her shoulders.

"Not at all."

"Must be Lord Whitehall, then."

"Lord Whitehall?" Cassandra scrunched her nose, confused.

"You were staring over in their direction. But you must have spent a great deal of time with Lord Covington as of late, which would have given you plenty of opportunity to appreciate him."

"Lord Covington?" she said, feigning nonchalance even as she realized she sounded like a parrot. "Yes, he has been at Castleton of course, and we have spent some time searching for the treasure since Gideon was called away, but I can assure you that nothing untoward has occurred between the two of us."

Which was a partial truth. Not entirely untoward. Not since they had arrived at Castleton. At least, not yet.

"If anything, I would say we are slowly learning to be friends more than enemies," she finished.

"Well, that is lovely," Hope said encouragingly, while Faith rolled her eyes.

"It is hard to believe that this ball came together so quickly, with your family having returned to the country so recently," Cassandra said, attempting to change the subject, and Hope allowed her to do so without comment.

"You know Mother," she said with a shrug. "Always needs to host an elaborate event before anyone else can."

"Now as for your riddle," Faith interjected, returning to their first topic of conversation, "I am beginning to believe that the author was not of sound mind. How could she have been, when no one has had the ability to make any sense of it?"

"That's just it," Cassandra said, biting her lip. "I wonder if she meant the clue for a certain person, one who would have particular knowledge to solve the riddle, knowledge that no one else would possess. But if neither Gideon nor I can make sense of it, then who could properly do so?"

"Perhaps there is no treasure at all, and this was all some old ancestor trying to lead her descendants on a chase while she gleefully cackles about it as she watches down on you," Faith said, causing both Hope and Cassandra to stare at her incredulously.

"Faith!" Hope finally exclaimed, but her sister merely shrugged.

"What? It is entirely possible."

"I suppose," Cassandra said reluctantly, knowing how much it would devastate Gideon if there was nothing at the end of all of this. In fact, she would be rather upset as well, for she was, at the moment, having great fun with it. Which had nothing to do with a certain Lord Covington, she told herself.

"Perhaps we can come help you search one of these days," Hope said, to which Cassandra smiled warmly.

"That would be lovely," she said, but they had to halt their conversation as a duo of gentlemen approached. They greeted all three ladies, but seemed to be known to Hope and Faith, and asked for their accompaniment in a dance. Cassandra could see that Hope was prepared to decline for her sake, but she waved her on, telling her not to worry, that she would find her own partner very soon.

Which happened much more quickly than she thought.

"Lady Cassandra, may I have this dance?"

She turned with a smile on her lips, although she was slightly surprised to find Lord Amberdash standing behind her. She knew him slightly through Gideon, but he did not frequent the same circles.

"Of course, my lord," she said, even though, truthfully, in her heart of hearts, she had been hoping that Devon would ask. But she noticed as she turned to look from the corner of her eye that he was still deep in conversation with Lord Whitehall and wasn't showing any indication that he had a care of what she was currently doing.

She placed her gloved hand in Lord Amberdash's, allowing him to lead her out onto the dance floor. She nearly groaned aloud when she realized that the current dance was a waltz, for she had no desire to be captured so close to him – but how was she to decline now without appearing appallingly rude?

Although perhaps another man's interest might coax Devon to pay slightly more attention to her. She was aware that she was acting in a rather spiteful fashion, but she couldn't seem to help her feelings.

"You look exceedingly becoming tonight, Lady Cassandra," the viscount murmured, his breath hot upon her ear, and she had to try not to shudder at his closeness. Why did another man's nearness bother her so when she welcomed Devon's proximity?

"Thank you," she said when she realized silence was growing between them. She was trying to recall if they had ever had much exchange before, but she couldn't remember such a time.

"Where is your brother this evening?"

"He was called away on business," she said, certain that Lord Amberdash likely already knew, for word travelled quickly as to the various whereabouts of guests who should have been in attendance.

"Leaving you alone – such a pity."

Cassandra turned her head sharply toward him, trying to determine just what was seeping out the edges of his voice.

"I can assure you that I am well looked after – and I am very adept at taking care of myself."

"I do not doubt it."

Cassandra didn't entirely enjoy the way she felt about him watching her through the remainder of the dance, but it wasn't as though she could say anything about it when he stood so close to her, his grip tight on her back and her hand. When the musicians finally brought the song to a close, she was quick to step back and curtsy before hurrying away to find her friends.

Unfortunately, Hope and Faith did not appear to be anywhere on the sides of the ballroom, and soon enough, Cassandra saw them out on the dance floor once more.

She spotted her mother with a group of women near the other end of the hall, but she had no desire to join them – she was sure their talk would be far too dull.

Instead, she decided that now would be an ideal time to find the ladies' room, and she slipped out of the ballroom to find her way.

She was pleased to be alone in the room – until she emerged to find a figure waiting for her in the shadows of the hall.

"Lady Cassandra, we meet again."

"Lord Amberdash," she said with some trepidation, looking one way and then the other, hoping that someone else would emerge. "What brings you to the ladies' retiring room? Perhaps you are lost?"

"Not at all, for I have found exactly what I am looking for. You," he said with a flourish, and Cassandra did not enjoy the predatory gaze he leered upon her.

"I can hardly think of any reason why you might have need to speak with me alone."

"Come now, Lady Cassandra," he said. "We all know of your propensity for scandal."

Cassandra stiffened. "You have heard incorrectly, my lord, for I have no interest in causing scandal," she said. "And I doubt you could possibly be aware of what has taken place in my past. However, I can assure you that it is nothing you need concern yourself with and has no bearing on my current regard for propriety."

"No?" he said, beginning to step toward her, and Cassandra looked around for an escape. Perhaps she could slip by him once he was close enough. "What if we create a scandal that no one has to know about?"

"I could not," she said, unable to help herself from taking a step backward for each he took toward her, but he continued to advance. As soon as he neared, she ducked under his arm, trying to hurry away from him and return to the ballroom.

Unfortunately, her skirts hampered her and before she could escape and emerge from the corridor, he had grabbed her arm and was pulling her backward.

"Unhand me," she commanded, but he leered down at her, wrenching her arm behind her back as he pulled her through one of the nearby open doorways.

"I will – in a moment," he sneered. "This should take but a

minute, as long as you behave. You know that everyone is aware of your true nature. There are few reasons why a young lady would be sent away as you were, only to return and not marry by a respectable age."

His words sliced through her, but at the moment, Cassandra didn't care what he had to say – her greater concern was regarding his actions. There were two potential consequences, each of which were very frightening – what he could do to her, and, even worse, the result if someone happened upon them. For she was sure, especially if his words were true, that no one would ever believe that she wanted no part in this. She would be well and truly ruined, and this time everyone would know who had done so. She would far rather have been forced into a union with Devon than this man.

Devon. Where was he, and what would he possibly think if he found them? He couldn't. She had to make sure of it. She needed to escape now.

"Lord Amberdash," she said, keeping her voice as even and calm as possible, "you are hurting my arm. Which I will need if we are to—" She swallowed, unable to finish the sentence, although her words had some desired effect, for he slightly loosened his grip as he swept an arm around her back and turned her to face him, now that they were in the confines of a small parlor, which was lit with a fire.

Cassandra'd had enough. In close quarters, she lifted her knee and drove it up between his legs. He let out a cry as he released her, and she managed to maneuver around him toward the doorway before he caught up to her, this time grabbing her hair, causing her to let out a cry she was unable to contain.

"You little wench," he snarled, and she closed her eyes as her head remained backward, except suddenly she was free and nearly falling forward from the quick change in momentum – into a broad chest. Her eyes flew open as familiar hands gripped her close, and she knew from his scent and the feel of his chest beneath her fingertips just who had arrived. It was exactly as she had feared, and yet, it was also how she knew she was safe.

"Devon," she sighed, leaning into him, and he murmured, "are you all right?" in her ear. When she nodded, he grunted, "good," before gently letting her go and moving her beside him.

"What," he said, growling out the words, "do you think you are doing?"

She opened her mouth to reply, until she saw that he was not addressing her, but instead was advancing on Lord Amberdash now, who was holding his head and chin high, although he was now the one backing up across the room.

"You know Lady Cassandra," the viscount said, waving a hand in the air, although his eyes were twitching from one side to the other, "always looking for a good time. I was going to give her one."

"You best think again before you repeat those words to *anyone*," Devon snarled. "She is a lady. *Lady* Cassandra. She deserves respect and has no interest in anything else from you. If you ever – *ever* – touch her again, then I will break every bone in your body, do you understand me?"

Lord Amberdash's jaw dropped open in surprise, as he began stammering, "b-b-but, I, she—" Suddenly his eyes narrowed. "She's your whore, isn't she?"

That seemed to cross the line for Devon, as he cocked his arm back and let his fist fly, right into Lord Amberdash's nose. Cassandra couldn't help but cringe at the sickening crunch, as much as she felt that the man completely deserved it.

"There is more where that came from," Devon said. "And that is just from me. Wait until her brother returns."

At that, he left the man and walked toward Cassandra, wrapping an arm around her shoulders.

"Come," he said. "Time to go."

Cassandra had never been so grateful as she sagged into him and allowed him to lead her away.

CHAPTER 13

*D*evon was doing all he could to hold himself in
control. He did not often lose his temper nor
resort to rage – he far preferred to deal with most circumstances with honey rather than vinegar – but what Lord
Amberdash had been about to do to Cassandra had pushed
him beyond any anger he had ever felt before.

"Devon," Cassandra was saying, her hand urgently
tapping on his arm. "Devon, can you slow down?"

He looked down and then around him, as though just
realizing their current setting, before he took them through
another door into what appeared to be a library. There were
a few other people within, speaking in small groups. Devon
nodded to them before leading Cassandra over to two chairs
in front of the fireplace. Here they would be able to speak
without risking being caught in a position that would, once
again, be considered improper, yet would also provide
Cassandra a few moments to compose herself before they
returned to the ballroom.

He couldn't look at her just yet, for the thought of what
could have happened had him seething all over again.

Instead, he took a few breaths, trying to calm his rage and rapidly beating heart.

"Devon, it's fine," she was saying once more. "Nothing happened."

"No," he finally managed. "Nothing happened. But what *could* have happened…"

"I know," she said, and he finally looked over at her. Her gaze was upon her hands, until she seemed to realize how she must look, and she reached up to fix the pins in her hair.

"Are you sure you are fine? Would you like me to find your friends? Or your mother? Or your maid so that you can retire? Or—"

"No," she said, finished with her hair, and she looked up at him now, meeting his eyes. "Just stay with me, please."

"Of course," he said, knowing that even if she hadn't asked it of him, he wouldn't have been able to tear himself away, for he would be too concerned that something else would threaten her. While he knew it wasn't her fault, she seemed to attract danger wherever she went.

"Devon," she said in a small voice, "is what he said true? Does everyone see me as a woman with loose morals woman? I know that there is some scandal attached to my name, made more difficult by my father's situation, but I wasn't aware that everyone thought such of me."

He was silent for a moment, uncertain of how to answer the question, finally deciding that honesty was the best policy.

"I had heard nothing except now I understand that some people speculate that there was more to your being sent away than what your mother and Gideon shared with others, which was that you were staying in Bath with your aunt," he said. "My suspicion would be that someone took a small speculation and turned it into a much larger rumor. Perhaps an enemy or one of the gentlemen you turned down when they asked for your hand."

"You have heard of that, then, have you?"

"I have now," he confirmed. "Whitehall informed me while we played billiards."

"If I had been found with Lord Amberdash by anyone else, the consequences could have been—"

"Dire," he finished. "Very dire. He certainly would not have been a man to provide any other explanation. He is one of those who hungers for power, who would do anything to be part of the family of a duke, to possess the influence that might come along with that. I imagine that was what drove him to seek you out."

"I am not sure if I should be insulted or relieved that this had more to do with his yearning for position than with me," she said wryly. "Still, I must thank you, Devon – not only for finding me, but for understanding that I wanted nothing to do with the man nor his… attempts."

He sat back to get a better look at her, blinking.

"Why would I ever think that?"

She shrugged. "Most people believe what they see without providing me a chance to explain."

"As happened to you before."

She nodded slightly. "I must admit, one of the reasons I was trying so desperately to get away from him was worry about what you might think if you learned what had happened, or *was* happening. I didn't know if you—"

"Stop," he said, though he tried to keep the word soft and not at all authoritative. "I would never think such a thing."

"But out of anyone, you are the only one who knows what I did—"

"And I also know that it happened between you and I because we wanted one another, not because you were seeking out a liaison with just any man, nor would you again."

Her lashes dipped low over her eyes again. "You are right about that. I would never—that is, no one else—I have no affection…"

Devon reached out and placed his hands over top of hers. "I know. I feel the same."

They stayed like that for a moment, until Devon remembered that they were not alone in the room – which was just as well, for he was sure that if they had been, he would have taken this a step further than he should, especially considering what had just occurred.

She cleared her throat. "I think we should find Hope and Faith now. They will have wondered as to where I have gone, to say nothing of my mother."

"Although she doesn't seem to have any suspicions when it comes to me, now does she?" he asked with a wry chuckle. "I suppose there will be a surprise in store, then."

He saw her head snap up at that, realized that perhaps he had given away a hint of his plan too early, but there was nothing to be done about it now. Instead, he rose, held his elbow out toward her, and escorted her back to the ballroom.

"Are you sure you would like to return?" he asked. "If you would prefer to excuse yourself, I'm sure we can locate your maid."

"That does sound like an attractive option, but I should tell Hope and Faith that I am retiring for the night first, at least," she said.

Devon nodded, although his attention was not completely on her as he kept his eyes open and searching for any sign of Lord Amberdash. Fortunately, the viscount was nowhere to be found, and Devon could only hope that he had done them all a favor and left the party entirely.

"How did you know where I was?" she asked as they approached the entrance of the ballroom.

"I noticed that you had left the ballroom and hadn't returned, which made me nervous," he said. "So I went searching for you."

"Good thing you did," she said fervently.

"I should have come quicker."

"It was quick enough," she said, patting his arm where her hand was already resting. "There are Hope and Faith," she said, jutting her chin toward them on the other side of the ballroom. "I shall return to them and explain some of what happened, although I will not share all of the sordid details."

"Perhaps you should," he said. "People should know what kind of man Lord Amberdash is."

She looked up quickly toward him in supplication. "Please don't tell anyone of what happened."

"Why not?" he asked, furrowing his brows. "The more that people know of what men like him can be capable of, the more it can be prevented."

"Because… what if it is as he says and people truly think this of me? I will be the one to be blamed, not him. That is the way of it, unfortunately."

He knew she was right, as much as he hated it. At the end of the day, it was her choice, and who was he to comment upon her decision?

"Very well," he relented with a dip of his head toward her. "Return to your friends, and when it is time to go to your bedchamber for the night, make sure you walk with someone you can trust."

"Like you?" she asked with a sly smile, but he took the answer very seriously.

"Exactly like me," he said, even though he hardly trusted himself in such close quarters with her. "Now, if your friends dance again, then I will be there to join you, understand?"

"Completely," she said, releasing his arm and turning to look at him. "Thank you, Devon. For everything."

"Of course," he said. "Anything for you."

* * *

"Cassandra, we were becoming worried about you," Hope said as she rejoined them. Cassandra didn't miss Faith's stare behind her toward Devon as he walked away, especially as Cassandra could still feel his eyes on her back.

"All is fine," she said. "At least it is now."

"Your sojourn away from the ballroom didn't have anything to do with a certain Lord Covington, now did it?" Faith asked, to which Cassandra shook her head.

"Not at all," she said, drawing a breath. "In fact, it is because of him that all is fine."

"What do you mean?" Hope asked with some consternation.

Cassandra hesitated. She hadn't wanted anyone to know of what had happened, but Devon's words resonated with her. She knew her friends would believe her, and she could prevent the same from ever happening to them.

"What I tell you, can it please stay between us?" she asked, and they both nodded.

"Of course," Faith said.

Cassandra proceeded to tell them most of what had happened, noting their gasps of shock and outrage.

"I shall tell Mother," Faith said, indignation taking over her expression. "She will make sure that he never shows his face here again. In fact—"

"No," Cassandra shook her head. "Please don't. That would just make everything worse. For it appears that most already think I am something of a… of a …"

Hope held up a hand, shaking her head. "Do not say it,

Cassandra. Do not even think it, for it will only give them the satisfaction of believing they have affected you. You know what kind of a person you are, what matters, and what you are deserving of. We know it too."

Of course, they didn't know the full story, but the fact they believed in her certainly meant something.

"Thank you," she said softly, realizing, for the first time, that she didn't feel entirely like a fraud for agreeing with someone who didn't know the full story of her life. For she was not the type of woman to give herself freely to any man. She had given herself to Devon, and only him.

Would she do so again, knowing what she knew now? For even if she did once more, there was a very good chance he would leave her once more, that now he would think her to be a woman looking for fun with him again. And she wasn't sure she would be able to take another dismissal from him.

The question wasn't whether she wanted him. It was whether he wanted her in turn – and whether she could ever trust him again.

CHAPTER 14

*C*assandra didn't have the chance to speak to Devon
alone again until they returned to Castleton the
next day. Her mother had remained awake throughout the
carriage ride home, and fortunately, didn't seem to have any
suspicion that dramatics had occurred the night before.
Instead, she chattered on about who she had seen, the latest
gossip she had heard, what each guest was wearing, and the
other house parties she had been told to expect that summer.
She briefly commented on her own wish to one day host a
party again, but Cassandra knew she would never do so until
she felt that she could properly showcase Castleton once
more.

Both Cassandra and Gideon had invited friends from
time to time in the past, but nothing that could be considered
a formal house party – at least, not to her mother.

Cassandra had felt Devon's gaze upon her, had known
that he wanted to ask if she was all right, how she had slept,
whether or not she had seen Lord Amberdash again, but she
had just shaken her head slightly at him to tell him that all

was fine, and they would speak more once they returned to Castleton.

Now here they were. The journey had taken just a half day and they had left around noon, which meant that dinner would be prepared shortly. Cassandra, however, didn't think she could sit through another meal with Devon staring at her, silently asking her questions while neither of them could say what was truly on their minds.

One thing was for certain – he was, perhaps, not the man that she had thought he was. When she had told him her story of being found in dishabille and being sent away to the institution, he had seemed truly surprised, as though he hadn't been aware of all that had occurred. If he had been… would he have done anything different? And if she had given him the opportunity to speak to her afterward… just what would he have said?

She had just left her bedroom to seek him out before dinner when she heard the closing of another door down the hallway and she jumped when he turned the corner of the corridor, stopping abruptly at his sudden presence.

"Cassandra," he said, her name on his lips causing her toes to curl and her chest to warm.

"I was just coming to find you," she said, hoping her reaction wasn't obvious.

"Well, here I am," he said, walking toward her, reaching out and running a hand down her arm in a gesture that could not be misconstrued for anything besides affection. "Are you well?"

"I am."

"Truly?"

"Yes, thanks to you," she said, beginning to walk with him down the hall. "Did you happen to see Lord Amberdash again before we departed?"

"No," he said, his brow furrowing. "I am not sure whether

I am glad of it or disappointed. For I would have liked to have told him more of what I thought of his actions."

"I wonder though…"

"You wonder what?"

"Would he have tried such a thing with any woman, or just with me? I knew there was some scandal attached to my name, but I didn't know it was to the point that gentlemen would think I was interested in just anyone."

He sighed as he ran a hand through his hair. "The truth is, I had never heard such a thing, but then, all know how close I am with your brother, and no one would ever say it in his presence. I know you are not that woman, Cassandra, and I am also aware that I never should have done what I did. It makes me no better than damn Lord Amberdash."

She stopped, turning toward him, placing a hand on his arm. "You are nothing like him."

"No?" he raised a brow. "Did I not—"

"Cassandra, Lord Covington, already going down to dinner?" They turned together as Cassandra realized they were standing on the top of the landing, her mother below them at the bottom of the staircase.

Even as Cassandra smiled, she could feel it wobble on her face, for she had wanted a moment with Devon, to speak about what had happened and assure him that he most certainly was nothing like the vile viscount. She needed to know what was going through his mind, what he had thought of her after all that occurred.

There was also the fact that she wanted to make it very clear that she could have handled herself if she had been left alone to do so.

"Yes, Mother," Cassandra said as they descended and walked in to the dining room together. Her father was already sitting at the table. Devon followed her and as he pulled out a chair for her, she leaned up and whispered, "Meet me at the fountain tomorrow morning. I have an idea."

His single acknowledgement of her words was his nod, and then he continued to his own place, although she didn't miss the warmth in his eyes when he sat down and looked toward her, a warmth that seemed to radiate through her own chest and into her toes.

"Oh, I have a piece of news," Cassandra's mother announced, and they all turned to her expectantly. "I received a note that Gideon is to return soon. Isn't that wonderful?"

Cassandra forced a smile to her face, even as a strange part of her was left suspiciously bereft. For as much as she loved her brother, she was enjoying searching for the treasure – and she was enjoying it even more so with Devon by her side. Gideon's return would mean that Devon would once again be spending time with his friend, and she was sure the two of them would find many reasons to leave her out of the search. It would be like her childhood all over again.

Which gave her greater drive to find what they were looking for tomorrow. It was the one way she could be sure to stay a part of this – and to spend more time with the man she had finally realized she would never be rid of – in her heart or mind.

* * *

DESPITE CASSANDRA'S SMILE, Devon hadn't missed the look of disappointment that had crossed her face last night at dinner at the news of Gideon's return. Was it because she knew he would likely discourage her from continuing to search for the treasure? Or was it that she was certain it would mean an end to their time together?

Inwardly, he hoped the latter to be true, although he did not hold altogether the same concerns. For once Gideon returned, Devon could speak to him about what was truly on his mind – his desire to court Cassandra.

The sole problem was whether or not his friend would allow it to be.

Today, he was much more interested in Cassandra's thoughts regarding where they should now be searching. She had asked him to join her out of doors once more. They had already searched the gardens and part of the ruins. Perhaps there was more to the ruins she wanted to explore.

He walked through the gardens, finding her once again at the fountain, although this time she was perched on the edge, as though aware that this was where he would search her out.

"There you are," she said with a cheeky grin. "Took you long enough."

He arched a brow at her, although he couldn't keep the smile off his face from simply being in her presence. "Well, when a lady does not provide the time for such a meeting, it does make it rather difficult to accommodate her expectations."

"I suppose that makes some sense," she said, tilting her head to the side. "How curious are you about where I would like to search?"

"Very," he admitted.

"You do know Castleton has a small lake upon the grounds?"

"Of course," he said. "Gideon and I spent much time swimming within it during the summer months."

"Well, I don't know if you recall, but at one time there were small servant cottages built near the lake," she said. "They are no longer used – primarily because we do not have nearly as many servants – and they have sat empty for years.

But would it not make sense?" Her excitement was palpable in the air. "I thought the clue was leading us to the servants' quarters. My father and Gideon expected it to lead us out of doors. This would mean that both of us were partially correct."

Devon nodded his head slowly as he rubbed his chin. "It would be clever, although it seems so far from the estate."

She shrugged. "It is still within walking distance. That is all that matters, is it not?"

"I suppose," he said thoughtfully, considering that her idea actually made a great deal of sense. "Are you prepared to go now?"

"Of course," she said, following his eyes. "And yes, I have my very best walking boots on."

She stood and they began toward the lake side by side, although Devon hadn't held out a hand to lead her, which she seemed to appreciate. It was not necessary, and she would likely see it as no more than him believing he had to look after her again.

"About what you were saying regarding yourself and Lord Amberdash," she said, and Devon could feel his ire rising again at just hearing the man's name, especially coming off her lips. "You are nothing like him. Nothing. I told him multiple times I wanted nothing to do with him and, in fact, demanded that he unhand me and leave me be. Whereas with you... I demanded quite the opposite and, in fact, wanted what occurred just as much, if not more, than you did."

She looked up at him then, her cheeks flushed but her eyes clear. "Do you understand?"

"You make yourself very clear, my lady," he said, swallowing hard, for he couldn't help but wonder if she would still want him now with the same ferocity as she had previously felt.

He didn't ask, however, did not want to scare her off, and besides, they had come to a clearing that showcased the lake stretching out in front of them. It was a rare day when the sun was high in the sky, its rays glistening down upon the blue of the lake. The water was so inviting, Devon's memories of swimming within it so vivid, that he was tempted to strip down and dive into its depths.

But of course, that was not his purpose today, nor something he would do within Cassandra's presence, as forward as she may be.

"I often forget how beautiful it is out here," she said, echoing his thoughts, and he nodded, his eyes coming to rest on the structures on the other side of the lake.

"Those are the cottages?"

"They are," she said as they began to walk the old, yet still worn, path around the water. "I imagine they are checked on from time to time to ensure that no one has taken up residence within them, but I cannot foresee that they have been kept in much order with no groundskeeper or gamekeeper in residence."

"We shall soon find out," he said, although he was already on his guard at the thought there might be someone within – someone he would have to be sure to protect Cassandra from. He wished he had known of their destination, for he could have brought a weapon of some sort.

They reached the small cottages, and Devon made sure to take a quick look within each first, not telling Cassandra why for he was certain she would fight him on it. Satisfied that all three were empty, they decided they would begin looking on the outside before making their way within. Cassandra suggested they split up once more, but Devon again refused, and they carefully, silently, looked over the exterior of each cottage. They were built of wood with some stone, but they seemed to be quite sound, no cracks appearing, no crevices that could hold anything within nor hide any treasure.

"Do you think the treasure could be buried underground?" Cassandra asked, but Devon shook his head.

"That would require reference in the clue, would it not? How else would you be aware of where it was? No, I think not."

"Let's go inside, then," Cassandra said. "Perhaps there is something hidden underneath the floorboards."

"Perhaps," Devon said, as a tingle tickled his shoulders and he turned quickly to look back behind him. "Do you feel…"

"Do I feel what?" she asked, her expression unreadable.

"Nothing," he said, shaking his head. He had thought, for a moment, that they were being watched, but that was ridiculous. No one had any reason to be out here at Castleton, tracking their movements as they searched around a lake in the middle of nowhere.

He was being far too cautious – which was not at all like him.

But when it came to Cassandra, it seemed that nothing was as it usually was. He was another man altogether.

For she meant something – something that no one else ever had before. He just wasn't sure whether that would lead to his own happiness or heartbreak.

CHAPTER 15

⌘

The mustiness of the small cottage crept over Cassandra like a light dusting of snow when she crossed the threshold. Devon was at her back, and she wondered as to the feeling he had asked her about. Did he mean a sentiment between the two of them or a clue regarding the search?

She longed to know, and yet was too afraid to ask.

For the more time she spent with him, the more she was realizing that the Devon she had thought she had known was not the man he truly was. He wore a front that he presented to the world, one he likely didn't even realize he had placed upon himself.

It wasn't that his charming air was falsified, nor was the smile he wore when he glanced her way or greeted anyone else. It was that, deep within, there was a protector, a man who cared, who had profound thoughts, who had, she knew now, been as swept up in the moment as she had been that day, who perhaps didn't always have the easy, right words that she always assumed he did.

Spending time alone with him had made her see him in a

different light, and it was a light that was shining brilliantly upon him, one she wanted to enter along with him.

The one-room cottage held just a few pieces of furniture, rather dilapidated ones at that. There was a desk and chair in one corner, a bed in the other, a fireplace against the wall with a small galley next to it for cooking.

"What do you think?" Cassandra murmured as she ran her hand along the blanket covering the bed, surprised to find that it wasn't as dirty or as dusty as she would have guessed. "Would you live somewhere like this, if it meant you had the lake next to you, nature around you?"

She heard the thud of the door closing behind them, and the thought of the two of them captured alone in here together made her heart race.

"I suppose it might be nice to live such a simple existence, although it would be rather lonely," he mused.

"But what if it wasn't?" she asked, turning around to capture his gaze. "What if you were not alone but lived here with someone else?"

"It would be rather cramped quarters."

"True," she said, swallowing hard at the heated expression that overcame his eyes. "It would require sharing a bed."

"It would, wouldn't it?" he said, although in more of a statement than a question.

"How… different it would be from what we are used to," she finished, dipping her head so that she wouldn't be staring at him anymore, for she was uncertain how to continue on with this topic of conversation.

"Different is not always a bad thing," he said, his voice lowering even more so than it usually did, causing tingles to run up and down Cassandra's spine.

"No, I do not suppose it is," she said, as she wondered just whether or not she should pursue this moment of opportunity that had arisen, of the two of them alone, when no one else knew of their whereabouts.

But then Devon suddenly turned away from her, shattering the moment as he loudly opened up each desk drawer, searching within.

Cassandra took slow steps as she approached him from behind.

"Do you really think that something would be hidden in such plain sight?" she couldn't but ask, and he shrugged.

"Could be," he said, although she heard the hesitation in his voice, the increased pace of his breathing. She wondered if he was as aware of what was simmering between them as she was. It was what she wanted to further explore, although he seemed to have made his mind up and she certainly wasn't going to press, not if there was the chance she could be denied by him again.

"Perhaps there is a false bottom to a drawer," he said.

Cassandra instead searched around the bed, looking beneath it as well as tapping all of the floorboards to see if any were hollow.

After a thorough search of the room, one which was filled with so much tension between them that Cassandra had difficulty concentrating on anything else, they finally decided that they had exhausted any options here.

"Onto the next?" Cassandra asked, and Devon nodded.

"Onto the next."

They had just exited the cottage when a flash of color from across the lake caught Cassandra's eye, and she squinted to get a better look.

"Did you see that?" she asked, holding up a hand to stop Devon when he shut the door behind them and came to stand at her back.

"See what?"

"Over there, across the lake," she murmured, pointing to

where the trees were grouped together beyond the water. "Perhaps I am seeing things, but I swear I saw someone moving. The color was too bright to be an animal. Too vivid of a red."

She looked up at him, finding his face furrowed into a frown of concentration. "I do not see anything now, but that doesn't mean there is nothing out there," he said, and she was grateful that he hadn't labelled her vision imagination. "What do you think it was?"

"I think—ahh!"

She couldn't help her scream when she heard the crack in the air, one that sounded remarkably like – a gun shot? Then the tree beside them suddenly splintered, and it took Cassandra a moment to realize what was happening.

"Devon? Are we being—"

But he had obviously already realized their alarming circumstances, as he had wrapped a hand around her waist and pulled her in toward him. Then, with his arms tightly about her, he dropped them both to the ground and rolled them together down the small hill in front of them. Cassandra would have far preferred to have retreated deeper into the trees behind them, or better yet, into one of the cottages, but it seemed that Devon had acted without exactly thinking of where they could end up.

For now they were picking up speed down the slope, right toward—

"Devon, stop! We are going to—"

But it was too late. He tried to dig in his heels, but it was not enough to stop their momentum, and they continued on until the cold water splashed over their heads.

Cassandra tried not to cry out, not wanting to provide anyone their whereabouts, but it had been a long time since she had swum in this lake, and there was a reason they had never entered it this early in the year.

"Devon!" she called out as the shallow water splashed over them, although it quickly dropped away and she found her feet were barely meeting the bottom while her head was still breaking through the surface.

She didn't feel a moment of fear, however, for Devon was there the entire time, his arm around her, keeping her lifted and close to him.

"Are you all right?" he murmured in her ear, and she nodded her head against him, feeling the wet tendrils of hair stuck to her neck as she tried not to shiver, instead pressing her body against him for warmth.

"Are you?" she asked.

"Of course," he said as though it was a silly question, one which she could only snort at. She was just as good of a swimmer as he was. "Let me guess," he continued. "You used to follow us to the lake and swim as well?"

"I did, actually," she said, surprised that he would already know, but then, she supposed he was coming to know her as well as she was him. "Devon, did someone... *shoot* at us?"

He still held her within the water, even as she shivered and attempted to move them back toward shore.

"Stay for a moment," he said in her ear. "I know that it's cold, but we're hidden by the rushes around us. If someone *was* shooting at us, best we keep hidden."

"But why on earth would someone be shooting at *us?*" she asked. "Surely it was someone out hunting, was it not?"

"You do not think the timing and aim would be too much of a coincidence?" he asked. "I think I was right – we were being watched."

"But why—" She realized it then. "Someone else wants the treasure."

"Perhaps," he acknowledged. "Who else knows about it?"

"As far as I am aware, my friends and yours," she said. "But none of them would do us any harm." She scrunched up her nose and leaned back away from him so she could look him in the eye. "Would they?"

"I doubt it, although sometimes we don't know people as well as we believe we do."

Wasn't that the truth?

Cassandra nodded slowly, even as her teeth began to chatter and her body shivered in the cold. "H-how much longer do you think we must stay in here?"

"We should be able to rise now," he said, not completely releasing her but keeping a hand on the small of her back as they began to wade back in toward shore. They stayed low and somewhat crouched beside the bushes that ran along this part of the lake once they reached the shore. Cassandra realized that her pale pink gown likely stood out among the natural landscape, but there wasn't much she could do about it now.

She looked down at the gown as though it was its fault, which was when she realized that it wasn't just her whereabouts the material was giving away. As the rain had done the other day, the water from the lake had molded the dress against her body – and this time there was no hiding anything that was underneath.

"I cannot return like this," she said to Devon as she crossed her arms over her chest to cover what she had always decided was a rather imperfect bosom. As it was, Devon couldn't seem to look at her at the moment.

"No, you really cannot," he said, slipping the jacket off his body and wrapping it around her shoulders. "Come, let us see if we can dry out a bit in one of the cottages."

They entered the second one this time – Cassandra figured it made sense, might as well search another place while they were at it – and it appeared to be much the same as the first.

Devon had already crossed the room, his hand running

over the mantel above the fireplace until he came up with a tinderbox.

"Here we are," he said, bending over the fireplace and working at it for a few moments until the fire leapt in the grate.

"Been awhile since you lit a fire yourself, has it?" Cassandra couldn't help but tease, and he looked back at her with smouldering eyes.

"You would be so adept at it, would you?"

"I could be. You never gave me the chance to prove myself."

"Next time, then."

"Do you plan to be trapped in a cottage alone with me a second time?" she asked, looking up at him from beneath her lashes.

"That remains to be seen," he said, before turning from her and crossing to the window, looking out at the landscape beyond. "I don't see anyone out there anymore," he said. "Hopefully we can spend an hour or so drying off and then return."

"Do you think anyone will come looking for us?" she asked, and he shrugged.

"Not for me, unless you think your mother will send out a search party."

"Only if any of the servants alert her that I have been out of doors for this long," she said. "Although sometimes I return through the library, and they wouldn't have any idea of my whereabouts unless they have need to find me. I think we shall be fine until dinner. Mother was going to spend the afternoon with Father, so she wouldn't have any reason to seek me out."

"That's good," he said, before looking around, walking to the bed and stripping it of its two blankets. "I am unsure exactly how clean these are, but they appear to have been kept in relatively good condition. If you… remove your dress, you could hang it by the fire and try to dry it some while wrapping this around you."

She nodded. "Very well."

He turned around and faced the wall. "I will not look."

He held his shoulders so stiffly, his body so straight and tight that it took everything within Cassandra not to laugh.

"That is all well and good, but it does pose something of a problem," she said.

"Oh?" he said, his voice strained.

"How am I supposed to unfasten my buttons and remove my dress alone?"

"I… ah, never thought of that," he said. "I cannot say I am particularly familiar with female garments."

Cassandra continued to gaze at his back, noticed the way his hands curled and uncurled from their fists. "That's not what I would have guessed."

"Says the woman who is nothing like what others think or say about her."

"That is true," she said, looking down at her fingers. "But you actually have the freedom to do as you please."

"What was it you said to me?" he asked, dipping his head, his voice low and husky. "That you had no desire to pursue a connection with any other man?"

"Yes."

"What if it was the same for me?"

That caused Cassandra to freeze herself, her entire body tensing up. He couldn't possibly mean what she thought he meant… could he?

"You are not telling me that you… that you have not been with other women because of me."

Silence stretched between them.

"Are you?"

"Perhaps."

Cassandra found herself standing there with her mouth gaping open, for once completely uncertain about what to say.

"But Devon... it's been years."

"So it has."

"And you mean to tell me, that in all that time, you never... you didn't..."

He whirled around now, his eyes full of anguish as he stared at her.

"Have you?"

"Of course not," she managed.

"Well, then, why would it be any different for me?"

"Because I thought that you didn't want me, that it was all a game, that what we did was something you were accustomed to... to *doing* with women."

He walked slowly toward her now, his every step seeming in time with the pounding of her heart. He reached out and took her hands with his, his touch sending waves of shock through her body, warming the frigidness that was beginning to settle in.

"There is much you do not know," he said, his eyes intent on hers. "I can answer any questions you like – but first you must dry your gown so that you do not freeze on me. Understood?"

She nodded woodenly as she turned around, displaying her back to him.

"Help me?"

CHAPTER 16

*D*evon had just admitted more to this woman than
he ever had to anyone before.

It was something he had promised himself he would
never share with another. Not Gideon, nor any woman he
ever did happen to make love to, whenever that time might
come.

Most certainly never, ever to Cassandra.

Yet here he was, confessing the truth to her, as his fingers
rose and began to slowly free each of her buttons from their
entrappings.

Cassandra did things to him that no other woman could
ever match. He had held onto his feelings for her for years
now, hoping they would ebb over time, that he eventually
would feel for another what he felt for her, would find a way
to rid himself of the affections that had dug in when he was
not quite yet a man and had never since loosened their grip.

But instead, they were only tightening all the more, especially when she stood here, so close, so open, so willing to
allow him in, in more than just one way.

"There," he said, hearing the crack in his voice as he stood back from her, allowing her dress to gape open at the back. "Do you need anything else?"

"I don't think so," she said, shaking her head, and as she began to push the sleeves down her arms, he turned around now, promising himself that today, he would be a gentleman. Soon, Gideon would return and he could speak to him and do this the right way. He had waited this long. He could continue on as he had been.

"Devon?"

"Yes," he said, on almost a groan. There was, however, one small problem with his reasoning – before, Cassandra hadn't been standing before him, a package of temptation.

"The wet fabric is too tight. It's clinging to my arms. Do you think you could—"

"Of course."

Despite everything within him telling him that this was a bad idea, he turned back around and swallowed down all of the desire that was threatening to emerge as he pushed the sleeves down her arms as gently as he could.

She was right in that the fabric was quite stuck, but together, they managed to slide the dress down her body to the floor, leaving her standing before him in her undergarments. The translucent chemise showcased every curve of her body, and Devon found himself nearly helpless to step back and away.

She reached down, causing the fabric to cling to her bottom, and picked up the blanket, slinging it around her shoulders before she shimmied out of her chemise as well. Keeping his eyes averted, Devon bent and picked up both articles of clothing before crossing to the fireplace and hanging them in front of it.

"Hopefully between the fire and the relative warmth of the air, they should dry soon," he said, looking back to find her staring at him from over the old blanket.

"What's wrong?" he asked.

She gestured toward him in response. "What about you?"

"What *about* me?"

"Do you not need to dry your clothing as well?"

"I shall be fine," he said. For if he removed his clothing, they would lose any sense of restraint they had left.

"Devon," she said, tilting her head to the side. "Do you know how guilty I would feel if you were to catch your death from freezing due to an attempt at protecting my nonexistent modesty? Leave your breeches on but at least dry your shirt."

"Very well," he muttered, removing his top garments and pushing the other chair over in front of the fireplace to hang them upon it. "Better?"

"Much," she said, before taking a seat on the edge of the bed. "Now. You promised to answer some questions."

He ran a hand through his hair. He had, hadn't he? It had seemed like a good idea at the time.

Now, he wasn't so sure.

"What are you wondering about?" He leaned back against the wall, crossing his arms over his chest, in part to warm himself, and in part to keep himself somehow protected from her inquisition.

"How many women have you… have you… tupped?"

He couldn't help but grin at her use of the word, so contrary to what would come off the lips of most young ladies. For one small moment he wished that she was a more reserved woman who would never find it within herself to ask such a question – for then he wouldn't be in this predicament of having to answer it. But if that were so, then she wouldn't be Cassandra, and Cassandra was the woman he wanted, so unlike any other he had ever met.

"Must I answer?" he asked despite already knowing his fate, and she nodded.

"You said I could ask anything."

"So I did. Very well." He paused, unsure of how she would respond to the truth. "One."

She blinked, her expression otherwise unreadable. "One."

"Yes. One woman."

"But you... with me..."

"Yes. You."

"But—"

"But what?"

"But how can that be?" she asked, standing now and beginning to pace back and forth in agitation, the blanket trailing behind her like a cape. "I know we ladies are not supposed to speak of it, not supposed to know of what goes on, but I am well aware that young men are encouraged to have a great deal of... experiences. You cannot tell me that the one time with me was the only time you ever did such a thing. Besides, you seemed rather... experienced."

"Why, thank you," he said with a grin.

"Devon! Do not mock me."

"I am not mocking you. A gentleman appreciates being complimented for his 'experience.'"

She lifted a hand to rub her forehead, and in doing so, came perilously close to losing the blanket. Devon wasn't sure if he would prefer that it fall or remain where it was.

"But... why?"

It was one thing to tell her that he hadn't been with any other woman. Explaining *why* he hadn't been was something else entirely. For that would open up a conversation that he wasn't yet ready to have with her, that could lead to dangerous happenings all over again. Gideon was his closest friend in the entire world. To disrespect his sister not just once but twice... would be inexcusable.

Cassandra was watching him now with hooded eyes, and

Devon turned from her, walking to the fireplace to see if her dress had dried at all.

Of course, as it had been no more than a few minutes, it was still soaked in lake water.

"I am sorry that you are trapped here with me," he said instead.

She cocked her head as though trying to read into just what he was saying.

"This is not your fault," she said. "Why, are *you* upset to be here with me, alone?"

Her blue eyes flashed, and he knew there was more behind her words, more that he was desperate to discover.

"Do you still hate me?" he asked. "Do you still wish that I was gone from Castleton?"

"Yes," she lied, staring him straight in the eye. He saw her pupils dilate and noted her breath quicken, and his body answered her with his own desire flaring to life deep within his soul.

"Do you know, Cassandra, that when you lie to me, you only become more attractive?"

He stepped toward her now, even as she, likely without even realizing it, began to approach him.

"I am not lying," she lied again, but now her eyes were on his lips as she licked her own. She had stepped close enough that he could reach a hand up and brush her hair back away from her face.

"Can you prove it?" He was treading dangerous waters here, but this was the effect that Cassandra had on him. He was a man who enjoyed pushing the limits as it was, but she altogether crashed right through any barrier that was still standing.

"How would I do so?"

"Simple. I shall kiss you."

"Kiss me?"

"If you will allow me to," he amended, not wanting to force anything on her, especially after all that had happened with damn Amberdash. "We shall see if you respond or not. If you decide that I am as despicable as you claim I am, push me away and I will never try again."

And if she was truly repulsed by him... nor would he speak to Gideon about courting her. It was actually a most certain way to test whether or not she had any affectionate thought or feeling toward him, a test that made his heart hammer as he considered this could be the last time he would come this close to her. "I would then also provide you with the apology that you would deserve. However, if you *do* respond..."

Oh, what he could do if she responded in kind.

"Then what?" she asked, her eyes bright and glistening.

"Then we will have to come to an arrangement of sorts."

"An arrangement?" she echoed him, question in her eyes, but he didn't want to explain at the moment, had no wish to scare her away. "I'm not sure—"

"May I kiss you?" He interjected, not wanting to speak any further of his thoughts before he ascertained the truth of her affections.

"You may kiss me if—"

He took that as a yes, wrapping one arm around her waist and the blanket cocooning her, pulling her in as his lips crashed against hers, his tongue already stroking the seam of her mouth as he found himself intoxicated by just this first taste of her.

He waited for her to recoil, to push him away, to slap him, but she did none of that. Instead, she opened her lips to him, moaning as she wrapped her hands around his neck. He felt the blanket drop to the floor at their feet, but he didn't care, didn't open his eyes as he was too intent on delving his tongue into her mouth, tasting her, owning her, remembering all that she had been to him before and all that he hoped she would be again.

Her soft, pillowy breasts rested against his bare chest, his breeches the solitary piece of fabric that remained between his cock and her center. He shouldn't do this, he knew that, yet he also couldn't seem to bring himself to stop the kiss and release her. For if he let her go now, would she ever return to him again?

She was the one, whoever, who deepened the kiss, who began stroking her tongue against his. Her hands ran up and down the skin of his chest, hot and fiery, until they continued lower and grabbed him through his breeches.

He had told himself he was going to wait before approaching her again. He was going to speak to Gideon, to ask to court her, to do all that was proper and right, in the order that he was supposed to follow.

But when she touched him, he recognized what had been missing from his life, what he needed nearly as much as he needed to breathe.

He was an earl. One who had a great deal of responsibility, who had people who depended on him, who needed him to ensure that all was in order for their very living.

But none of that was about him. Any man within his lineage, including his very competent brother, could take his place and all could continue along as it had been.

Cassandra, however, could not be replaced. Cassandra was his, the one thing that made him different, who fit with him more than any other woman ever could. He could not imagine his life without her, didn't know what he would do if she ever turned him down or if Gideon told him that he wasn't fit to court her.

She didn't want him because he was an earl, or because he would be an advantageous match for her. In fact, she had done all in her power to avoid being alone with him. But here, now, she was with him because she wanted *him*, and no one else, which she had proven time and again when the opportunity had presented itself to her.

If only he had persisted years ago, had realized how important she was to him and how much he needed her in his life.

So much angst could have been avoided.

Instead, his inaction had served to create her hatred toward him, hatred that he now understood he deserved.

Sometimes, however, love and hatred were not so far apart.

As was evidenced by the fact that she was here, kissing him as though she was part of his soul, that despite the fact they shouldn't be doing this, not here, not now, they couldn't keep away from one another, their attraction as volatile as the gun outside.

Devon suddenly felt his lack of "experience" as Cassandra had continued to describe it, was catching up with him. He had no finesse, his charm seemingly vanished as he ran his hands up her body, cupping the underside of her breasts.

"You are irresistible," he murmured against her lips. "I do not know why or how you do this to me, but—"

He cut short his sentence as he was too focused on the strokes of her fingers over his chest, the flush of her neck and cheeks, the rapidness of her breathing, the size and darkness of her pupils as she leaned back and stared up at him.

"Does that kiss show you how very—" she took a deep breath, "—unaffected I am?"

He saw the smile tease her lips, knew that she was enjoying toying with him. "I would argue that you most certainly responded."

"Did I now?"

He growled low in his throat, leaning down and wrapping an arm beneath her knees. She let out a squeal as he lifted her in his arms and carried her over to the small bed that was now covered with just a thin blanket. He set her gently down upon it before leaning over her, holding himself up on his fists.

"You are unaffected, are you?" he asked, his nose just inches from hers, her lips reaching up toward him again. He could feel her breath on his cheek as her scent of fresh air and sunshine washed over him. Her lashes lowered, and he couldn't help but reach one hand up to cup her breast. His thumb teased her nipple which was already straining up toward him, and she gasped as she arched her chest into his touch.

"Completely… undaunted," she lied, even as her head tilted back, and her eyes closed while a smile danced over her lips.

"I thought we discussed never lying."

"*You* discussed it. I never agreed."

"What do you think I should do to punish you?"

"Punish me?" Her eyes widened at that as though she was initially angry at the thought, but then as she swept her eyes down over his bare chest to the bulge in his breeches, she seemed to forget what they were discussing. Her fingers followed the same path, over the muscles of his torso, until they were playing with his waistband. "Are you threatening me, my lord?"

"It depends upon how you feel about what I must do."

"Which is?"

He grinned. She had proven now that she wanted his touch as much as he needed hers, that she was not unaffected by him, and, in fact, likely didn't hate him at all.

She was his – even if she didn't quite know it yet.

"I am going to kiss you again."

CHAPTER 17

*T*hey shouldn't be doing this.

Not again.

They had made the mistake once before, and Cassandra had vowed to herself that she had learned her lesson. It wasn't because she thought this was wrong – how could it be when it felt so right – it was because of what had happened last time, of how she had been left alone to face the consequences as well as the loss of all she had known and all she had wished for.

Devon had seemed to be of the same mind – although likely for completely different reasons – but as bared to one another as they were, they couldn't seem to keep themselves away from one another.

"We shouldn't do this." She said it aloud now as though it might help put a stop to things, even as her actions betrayed her, for her hands were pulling his hips into her, longing to feel his straining erection against her center.

"We shouldn't," he agreed before pausing. "Although we have once before."

"We have."

He leaned down and teased his teeth over her plump bottom lip. Cassandra reached up with her legs, wrapping them around his hips and using them to pull him in toward her.

He left her lips for but a moment, but fortunately it was to lower them into the hollow between her breasts.

"You have the most beautiful breasts I've ever seen."

"Are they not the *only* breasts you've ever seen?"

"I never said that."

She gaped at him. "You've seen other breasts?"

He lifted his head, his eyes dark as he stared at her. "Would you like to discuss this now or would you like me to continue with what I am doing?"

She swallowed hard, annoyed at the jealousy it stirred within her to think of him anywhere near another naked woman, but she supposed there would be plenty of time to worry about that later. "Continue."

"I do not just want your breasts," he said, his voice guttural, his mouth in her neck. "I want all of you. From your head down to your toes. I want to be between your thighs. Your mouth on mine. I want to taste you and feel your heat around me."

"Oh my—" she couldn't finish her sentence when his tongue laved the space beneath her ear, and she couldn't keep her legs from tightening around him, pulling his hardness against the growing heat between her legs. She rocked against him, needing to feel his skin against her instead of his breeches, but she was unable to keep herself from moving in order to take more of what she wanted.

"Do you enjoy when I touch you here?" he asked as he took the weight of both of her breasts in his palms, circling her pink nipples with his thumbs, teasing her when he wouldn't touch the tips of them this time.

"Yes," she hissed. "More."

"What about here?" he asked, moving lower, his large hands and long fingers spanning her ribcage beneath her breasts.

"Yes."

"And here?" he continued as he slid his hands around her, cupping her backside, and she shifted against him again, feeling ever the wanton for being the one to ask him to continue but unable to stop her body from taking what he offered.

Finally, he shifted back away from her and released the fastening of his breeches. He leaned down and kissed her, not finishing the job of removing his clothing, so she worked her hands between them to do it for him.

Meanwhile she continued to kiss him, needing him more than she would ever want to admit to him, certainly, but even to herself.

"We shouldn't do this," she murmured again, and he leaned back away from her, his eyes intent upon hers.

"Tell me to stop, and I will. I promise you that. I will honor your wishes, but I will make you mine in spirit. And if you do not want me today, then tomorrow I will do all I can to prove I'm worthy of you. And the day after that. The week after that. The month after that. You are the only woman for me, and I will do all that is within my power to be the man for you, the man you need, the man you want, the man you love. I need you, Cassandra, with all of me, and no matter what it takes – as long as you say the word – I will have you."

Did he truly mean all of that or was he just trying to win her over with flattery? Cassandra lost the ability to breathe at his words, as his hand rose, gliding over her cheek to cup her face in his hand. She stared into the depths of his dark brown eyes, which seemed to now be full of promises, full of desire, full of everything she had thought she would never want from him but now wasn't sure how she could ever live without.

"My role as earl demands that I find an appropriate young woman to marry, to bear my children, to give me an heir as I work to fulfill my duty and destiny and look after all who are under my care. However, if you will not have me, there will be no other, just as there never was before. I cannot marry any young lady just because she might fit what society expects. I want only you. You are the woman who has captured my heart, my soul, my body, my affection."

Cassandra had no idea just what to say to such a profound declaration, how to match the poetry of his words, so instead she didn't say anything at all.

She pushed his breeches the rest of the way down as once again she took his mouth with hers, wrapped her legs around his waist, and pulled him down so that his bare cock was resting against her core.

He was here, with her, and she was going to take his promises, take what he offered, and, for once, believe in him. Trust him.

Even if she had told herself she never would again.

He pushed at her entrance, his crown finding itself home with her. Cassandra opened her legs wider, welcoming him in, as her hips thrust upward and her nails bit into his shoulders.

"Yes, Devon!" she cried out, and he pulled back and then kissed her neck as he reached down and stroked her bud of desire while she rocked into his hand.

He leaned his head down and took the tip of her breast into his mouth, and she couldn't help but lace her fingers into his hair as she held his head against her while his tongue swirled. Every sensation was working together to build her desire deep within, and she yearned to feel all of him, needed him back inside her.

"Please, Devon," she moaned, hating that she was begging but unable to form any other words.

"Do you like this?" he asked, ignoring her as he moved to the other breast.

"Yes, but—"

She jerked her hips up into him again as her hands gripped his shoulders so tightly she wondered if she would leave bruises upon them.

"What do you want from me?" he asked, his voice low and raspy. "Better yet, *how* do you want me? From behind? From above you? From beneath you?"

She gasped at the images his words provoked, positions that she hadn't known were possible, but now made her want to try all of them.

At the moment, however, she didn't have any preference as long as he was within her and was willing to allow him – just this one time, in this one situation – to take control.

"Any way," she said, reaching out and stroking his cock from top to bottom, deciding that the one way to have him get on with this was bringing him as close to the edge as she currently was. "As long as you get inside me *now*." He looked at her with an eyebrow cocked, and she sighed heavily before finally adding. "Please."

"Well, with such manners, how could I possibly resist?" he said with a grin that sent shivers down her spine. He surprised her by standing beside the bed, lifting her knees, and then sliding her forward before he positioned himself between her legs, leaning down to kiss her again as he pressed himself into her, finding home.

They rocked together, back and forth, skin against skin, Devon's gaze intent as he drove into her, over and over. It wasn't smooth, it wasn't finessed, but Cassandra didn't care. His need, his want for her was evident, and that meant more than anything else ever could.

"I'm sorry this is fast," he said, gasping hard, and she shook her head as her hips rose and fell, meeting his.

"I do not care," she said as sensation began to build in her, sensation that she couldn't hold back, that she didn't want to prevent. "I want you, and that is all. *Devon.*"

She cried his name as she began to pulse from deep within, pulses that radiated through her body, driving her mad. It must have triggered his own climax as his eyes closed and he bucked within her, once, twice, the waves of pleasure so intense that Cassandra never wanted it to end.

Finally they both stilled, stopping and staring at one another in wonder.

"Cassandra," he said, leaning down toward her, stroking her cheek. "That was… that was… everything."

She nodded slowly, her head jerking into his touch.

"*You* are everything," he said, his words all that she would have wanted to hear the first time they had come together, words that she had never received from him.

Only now could she finally admit that part of the reason the words had never come was because she hadn't allowed him to share them with her once he asked for the chance.

He eased down off his hands, coming to rest beside her instead, propping his head up on his hand as he stared at her. Seeming to read her thoughts, he continued. "Last time, I didn't tell you how I felt, was too afraid to let you know what you did to me. But the truth is, Cassandra," he ran a hand down her arm, "I do not want this to be the last time we are together. I want… more. I want… you."

She wished, for a moment, that they could stay in this small cottage forever, that the dream of living here, alone with just the lake and nature around them for background, could come true.

But of course, this was but a moment in time. There were brothers, families, treasures, responsibilities to consider.

"Your brother returns tomorrow," he said slowly, and Cassandra's heart jumped as she was already shaking her head.

"No," she said.

"You do not even know yet what I am going to say."

"You will not tell him of this. Nor of the time before."

Devon was silent for a moment. "I am not sure that we should continue lying to him."

"Not telling him something is not the same as lying to him."

"Isn't it, though?" he questioned uneasily. "Honestly, Cassandra, I do not know how I can continue to be around you and pretend as though I feel nothing for you. I know that your emotion toward me was far from affectionate, but I do hope something has changed."

Of course it had. Everything had changed – most of all, Cassandra's own realization that what she had felt for Devon all this time was not necessarily the hate she'd thought it had been. No, instead it had been something else entirely. She had been so wrapped up in funneling all of her emotion into the fact that he had left her without a word that she hadn't stopped to consider just *why* it had bothered her so much.

It was because she had cared for him more than she had ever admitted.

"If Gideon knows what happened between the two of us – now or before – he would never forgive us. Especially you," she said, reaching out and placing a hand over his heart to soften her words. "I know how much your friendship means to both of you. I would hate to be the cause of any discord. It is better that he never know of it."

Devon was silent for a moment, the only response the ticking of his eye.

"Very well," he said with some resignation. "But that does

142

not mean that I will not be speaking to him about you. And us. And my intentions toward you."

"Which are?" she asked, raising a brow.

"That I mean to do right by you, Cassandra. And not just because we have now been together once more and, yet again, there is the possibility of a child growing between us. It is because I cannot see my life without you. Do you understand?"

This had all happened so quickly, the change so abrupt, that Cassandra's first inkling was to say no, this couldn't be, she couldn't have her life upended like this.

But then she looked at Devon, at how he returned her stare, and she knew that if she allowed him to walk away now, she might never have him again.

Just a few weeks ago she would have accepted such a situation – in fact, she would have embraced it. But now… now the thought of being without him was utterly unfathomable.

"I understand," she said slowly to him. "But Devon?"

"Yes?"

"Perhaps do not say anything right away. We have been here at Castleton for a fortnight, alone together except for my mother, who has been completely oblivious to anything occurring between us, and my father, who believes us to be married anyway. Gideon would know that something has occurred, would he not?"

"He might guess that my feelings have grown for you, but I do not believe he would ever have expected me to act upon them."

"Nor me," she said before grinning at him. "We are rather misbehaved, are we not? Perhaps you have corrupted me."

"Or you me."

"Why do we not begin by showing him that we no longer despise one another? That, at least, we are friends?"

He leaned in and kissed her on the nose in a gesture so

gentle and affectionate that she nearly teared up once more. "I promise you, Cassandra, friends we will always be – among everything else."

"You are something else, Lord Covington," she whispered, no longer able to prevent moisture from welling in her eyes. "Something else indeed."

CHAPTER 18

*D*evon dearly wished that he hadn't promised Cassandra not to share his intentions with Gideon just yet. He agreed with her that leading with the fact he had compromised her might not be the method to ensuring her brother's agreement to their courtship. However, he would have liked to be able to make his purpose known sooner rather than later.

His friend arrived the next day, pleased to have returned and eager for news on their search.

They were sitting around the table in the drawing room, prepared to have a discussion, and Devon couldn't remove his eyes from Cassandra. Her eyes flicked over to him now and then and at one point, she shook her head with a frown, likely convinced that his gaze was going to draw Gideon's attention, but Devon couldn't find it within himself to care.

He wondered why she did so overly much.

"So you have made no progress?" Gideon asked.

Cassandra frowned at him, and Devon lifted his tea cup to his lips, taking a sip before he answered.

"I wouldn't say that," he said. "We have, at the very least, determined where the treasure is *not*. It is not in the long gallery. It is not in the ruins. It is not in the gardens. And it is not in the old servants' quarters across the lake."

"I never thought of searching there," Gideon admitted, leaning back and crossing one leg over his other knee. "Actually, that seems like a rather natural answer to the riddle."

"It does, doesn't it?" Cassandra said, pleasure lighting her face.

"It was Cass—Lady Cassandra's idea," Devon added, which caused Cassandra to frown at him once more. Goodness, was her intention to the do the exact opposite of showing her affection? If she wanted to convince her brother that she continued to hate him, she was doing a rather fine job of it. Meanwhile, Devon had thought their plan was to show that he was beginning to grow on her, that they had decided to become, at the very least, friends.

"You always were the clever one," Gideon admitted. "I have been asking that the cottages be kept as clean as possible, in case we are soon in the fortunate position that we can afford to hire more servants. They haven't been lived in for quite some time, however. What were the results of your search?"

Devon couldn't help now but look over at Cassandra, seeing the red flush creep up her cheeks, and it took everything within his power to hide his grin.

Cassandra opened her mouth a couple of times but couldn't seem to find the right words. Devon decided it was up to him to do his best to respond. "It was productive," he said with a smile. "We were very thorough. Nothing was left untouched."

Cassandra had lifted her teacup to her mouth, likely in order to hide her face, and now she began sputtering, choking on her tea. Devon, who had taken a seat next to her on the sofa – although not so close to be suspicious – patted her on the back, gliding his hand between her shoulder blades between pats.

"I say, Cassandra, are you all right?" Gideon asked, and she nodded, although her face was still rather screwed up in consternation.

"Just fine," she choked out, and it took everything within Devon not to laugh.

"As you were saying?" Gideon said, turning to him once more, and Devon attempted to sober.

"Despite our very best efforts, we were unable to find the treasure we were looking for," he said, pausing for a moment. "However, there was another occurrence of note."

Cassandra's head snapped up at that, as she stared at him with daggers in her eyes. "Devon—"

"We believe we might have been shot at," he finished, and she sagged back into her seat at his words.

"You *what?*" Gideon said, coming to his feet. "Why would you think such a thing? Are you certain?"

"Not entirely," Devon said, shaking his head. "We had just left one of the cottages when Cassandra thought she saw a colorful motion across the lake. She did immediately believe that it was a person."

"The color was too vibrant to belong to nature," she said, and Devon nodded.

"Then we heard a crack that sounded like gunfire, and a second later the tree next to us splintered from being hit. There is certainly the chance that someone was out hunting, but why shoot at us, over by the cottages?"

"Unless whoever it was thought that you were an animal, and then upon realizing their mistake, hid so that they wouldn't be blamed."

"It is possible," Devon conceded, although he believed it had been too close to have been such a coincidence, "but we thought we should note it for you." He paused for a moment.

"We had one other question for you. We inventoried and searched the statues in the long gallery but were not sure if anything was out of place. Do you have a list yourself?"

"I do," Gideon said with a nod, opening a drawer and looking through his desk. "Here it is."

Cassandra took the paper from him, opening her notebook and beginning to review each list. They spoke of Gideon's visit while they waited, until finally Cassandra sighed, shaking her head.

"Nothing appears out of the ordinary."

"Another idea to cross off the list," Gideon said, scratching his jaw. "I have been thinking more about the riddle."

"Have you solved anything?" Cassandra asked, her expression a mixture of hope and disappointment, likely hope for a lead and disappointment if her brother had solved something before she did.

"No, but I have some ideas," he said.

"I'm guessing you do not want to share them with me?" Cassandra said, arching a brow.

"I do," Gideon said, even though it was very clear that he didn't. "And I will. It is just—"

"What?"

"Nothing."

"Gideon," Cassandra said threateningly, her teeth ground together, "what is it?"

"I just believe it might be in your own best interests that Devon and I pursue this. Without you."

"Is that not for me to decide?" she asked, obviously entirely displeased with her brother.

"It is only that — through absolutely no fault of your own — trouble seems to... follow you. Or find you. I'm not sure which," Gideon admitted, wincing as he did so.

Cassandra's jaw dropped open, even as Devon was

already sitting forward on the sofa as the need to defend her rose within him.

"Now, Gideon," he began, but Cassandra eyed him with a look that told him not to interfere any further.

"How can you say such a thing?" she asked. "Trouble doesn't *follow* me. I just—I simply—"

Gideon leaned forward and placed a hand on her knee. "It's like being shot at while searching the cottages. That wasn't your fault, and yet, it happened. Did anything else occur at other times when you were searching?"

"Not really," Cassandra said with a shrug, although her lie was obvious by the flare of her nostrils. "Just a bit of rain outside and some contrary statues in the long gallery."

"And Devon told me what happened at Lord and Lady Embury's. That you were nearly accosted just outside the ballroom."

Cassandra turned to Devon with a murderous glare, but he didn't feel any regret.

"He had to know about Amberdash," Devon said defensively. "We can hardly invite the man into our circles now. He must be punished, and the best way to do so is to make him feel a social outcast."

Cassandra had set her teacup down and now crossed her arms over her chest, clearly feeling attacked.

"Just think of that business a few years ago, that had you sent away," Gideon said, and now Devon could feel the beginning of a headache at his temples. "You obviously didn't do that to yourself, and yet you were the one who was chastised. Trouble is attracted to you, Cassandra. As are, obviously, gentlemen who should know otherwise than to attempt ruining a young lady."

Of course, Gideon could hardly be aware of it, but that last remark was directed at none other than Devon himself, as he was the one who had properly ruined Cassandra – twice now.

"I am not keeping anything from you out of some punishment or anything of the sort," Gideon said. "Rather, I am just trying to protect you."

"I can protect *myself*, thank you very much," Cassandra said, not hiding the malice in her voice.

"I know you can," Gideon said slowly, and even Devon had to cringe at how patronizing his tone was. "But there are times when I must do so as well. It is part of my role – as your brother and as the head of this family."

Devon could tell that there was much Cassandra wanted to say to that as she ground her jaw and clenched her hands in and out of fists, but she refrained, likely because she knew that to argue would surely make Gideon more inclined to believe she couldn't look after herself.

Cassandra took an audible breath, in and out, and Devon knew exactly what she was thinking – that if she was not allowed to continue to search with the two of them, she would only do so alone, which would likely lead her into more trouble than he could imagine.

"Very well," she said, her smile towards Gideon icy, and Devon was glad that her ire was not directed at him. "If that is what you would prefer."

"Cassandra—"

"Since we are going to be out here in the country for a while, Gideon, I believe I would like to invite my friends to join us."

Gideon's eyes widened. "All of them?"

"Yes, all four. Just for a time. It will be a fun house party."

"I am not sure—"

"We could make a few days of it," Devon interjected with a smile, attempting to find a way to assist Cassandra without making it overly obvious – to her or to her brother. "Perhaps

Ferrington and his brother would join. Whitehall is already nearby. He was at Embury's house party."

"Was he now?"

Devon nodded.

"I'm not sure that Mother would be pleased with the idea," Gideon said, frowning. "She doesn't feel the house is fit to host as of right now."

Cassandra frowned crossly at him. "They have all been here before, at one time or another. Just never all at once. Besides, they all know of the treasure and can help the search. And do you not think it would be good for Mother to have people in the house again? She used to love hosting."

"But that was before Father... and speaking of him—"

"All of our friends know of his circumstance. It might do him well to have more people around again, even if he is not entirely aware who they all are."

Gideon sighed as he rubbed his forehead, but Devon could see that he seemed already resigned to what his sister was suggesting.

"Very well," he said. "Invite them."

"Truly?" Cassandra asked, her face alighting.

"But *you* are going to be the one to share the news with Mother."

"I can handle Mother," Cassandra said with a sly smile. "Besides, Gideon, did you not just tell me that *you* are the head of this household?"

Devon couldn't help but grin at her cheek, and even Gideon had to laugh at her cleverness.

"Sometimes, Cassandra, I wonder what I am going to do with you."

Fortunately, Devon had the answer for that. He just needed time to make it known.

CHAPTER 19

*C*assandra loved her brother. Truly she did. But sometimes, he was a bit of a pompous ass. She knew that he was just trying to do what he thought was best. It was about time, however, that he realized that she was a grown woman who could make her own choices; who, if trouble so often found her as he claimed, could find her way out of it by herself, thank you very much.

But she knew if she argued with him, it would only be proving his point, that he thought she needed the assistance. And so instead she decided she would simply do as she pleased – with or without his permission.

They sat around the breakfast table the next morning – Cassandra, Gideon, Devon, and her mother, as her father had not yet joined them.

"Mother," Cassandra began. "I am going to invite a few friends out to visit."

"So soon?" her mother asked with some dismay. "We only just opened up Castleton. I had been hoping to hire more servants, but Gideon wasn't yet sure…"

"It's fine. Hire a few more, if you'd like," Gideon said, waving a fork in the air.

"Can we afford it?"

"A few maids, yes," he said. "No more footmen than what we already have."

"That should help somewhat," his mother said, contemplating the idea. "Especially if the women visiting bring their own ladies' maids. We would need the most help in the kitchens and preparing the bedrooms. How many shall there be?"

"Hope and Faith, as well as Madeline and Persephone. I expect they will each bring a chaperone as well."

"Oh, that is quite a few," her mother said, tapping her finger on her chin as her lips dipped at the corners.

"It will just be for a couple of nights," Cassandra said. "Hope and Faith live so close that it will be but a half day's journey for them. The others may need slightly longer if they are coming from farther away."

"Well," her mother said, though she seemed somewhat chagrined. "I suppose they have seen the state of Castleton before."

"It truly is a lovely home, Your Grace, with plenty of character," Devon chimed in, his voice low and comforting, and Cassandra felt heat in her face simply at the fact that him speaking affected her so. Goodness, what was becoming of her? "I find it holds a great deal of charm and I always feel welcome here, which is what is most important, is it not?"

Her mother smiled at him. "I suppose so. You are too kind, Lord Covington."

"I speak only the truth."

And he did, didn't he? That was one thing that could be said for Devon.

"As it happens, I might have a few guests myself, Mother,"

Gideon said, clearing his throat, and at that their mother began shaking her head.

"I do not know about that, Gideon. The gentlemen will have estates that are much grander and when they see Castleton, what might they think of—"

Cassandra cleared her throat and mouthed to Gideon, "head of household." He rolled his eyes at her, but seemed to be slightly more encouraged to stand his ground.

"It will be fine, Mother," he said firmly, and Cassandra nodded her approval at him. She understood why he looked to their mother for guidance, having been quite young when he had to take over the household responsibilities once they had realized their father was no longer competent. But Gideon was now more than capable, and a grown man at that. He should not need his mother's approval for every action he took.

"Very well," her mother said with a sigh, although there were worry lines between her eyes now, lines that made Cassandra feel slightly guilty for having pushed this all forward. But if they were going to find this treasure, they might as well do so together, and it was obvious that Gideon was not going to include her in the search unless she took some control over the situation herself. "How soon will it be?"

"We shall send the invitations today," Cassandra said. "And invite everyone to arrive in a week's time."

"A week? That is hardly enough time to prepare the house, and your father—"

"Both the house and Father will be fine," Gideon said, cutting her off. "Besides, it will be good for both you and Father to have plenty of people around again. As it was in the old days."

"Yes," their mother said, her eyes taking on that far away, reminiscent look. "Yes, I suppose it just might be."

After their breakfast concluded, Cassandra retreated to the sitting room to write her invitations, doing so for Gideon as well. It was where Devon found her a short time later. He took a seat on the sofa next to her, lounging upon it.

"Sometimes you scare me," he said in a low voice, and she looked up to see him watching her, although there was humour in his eyes.

"How so?" she asked.

"By how you so easily manage to get your way."

She stopped then, slightly hurt as she looked up at him. "Are you calling me manipulative?"

She knew she sometimes had to go about things indirectly, but it was not easy as a woman – especially when her brother had other ideas entirely and wouldn't listen to her opinions.

"Not at all," Devon said, shaking his head. "I believe you have a great deal of ingenuity, as it were. I'm just not sure that your brother and your mother realize how well you know them and are aware of what to say to convince them to see things your way."

Cassandra nodded slowly. "I only want what is best – for all of us." She paused, uncertain about how to ask Devon what had been bothering her since their conversation with Gideon. "Do you agree with Gideon? That I find trouble wherever I go? For I do not mean to. Not at all." She lifted her arms by her side. "When the gentlemen approach with their comments and propositions, I do not ask for their attention, nor did I think they knew that there had been an… indiscretion in the past. Yet sometimes I feel as if someone has written on my back, 'open for attention.'"

Devon paused for a moment, his dark eyes hard and assessing as he stared at her. "You are a beautiful woman, that much is for certain."

Cassandra waited, for she knew there was more. She was

aware that she was decent enough looking, but she was not an incredible beauty such as Hope, who suffered none of the same issues as Cassandra did.

"You have a quality about you," he said slowly. "An attractiveness that is hard to deny. A charm, perhaps, might be the best way to phrase it, with an impishness that suggests you just might be open to not care about what is expected of you."

"I see," Cassandra said, uncertain of how she felt that he would think such of her. When she spoke again, she was chagrined to find that her voice was just above a whisper, but she almost didn't want to ask the question for fear of what his answer might be. "Did you believe that of me, especially the night we were together? Is that why you wanted me?"

"No," he said, sitting up from his lounged position to look directly into her eyes. "I didn't suspect any of that, because I already knew you. I knew who you were, what was in your soul, and I certainly never meant for things to go as far as they did. All I wanted that night was to tell you what I felt for you, what I had *always* felt for you. Instead, I ended up showing you, and it all ended up coming back to slap me in the face. It would have been much better had I simply told you how I felt first. Then you would never have wondered whether or not what happened between us had any meaning."

She nodded, tears prickling the back of her eyes.

"This is why I do not want what we feel for one another to be kept secret any longer," Devon continued. "If others were aware that I was courting you, perhaps no one would be inclined to have any reason to think you might be... accepting of their affections."

That had Cassandra's spine stiffening. "I should not need to be possessed by a man for there to be any question as to whether or not I am some kind of trollop."

"I never meant that," he said with a sigh, and she knew what he was thinking – that she was making this difficult for him, always putting up barriers. But, above anything, she had to protect her heart. And as much as she did have feelings for Devon, she still had to know that he would allow her to be her own woman, that he wanted her for her, that there would never be the opportunity for him to leave her again.

"I know," she said, taking some pity on him. "I just want to be able to make my own choices and to be seen for myself rather than who I am in relation to my brother or the man I might one day marry."

He looked at her with some pity, and she knew exactly what that expression meant – that she was a fool for thinking such a thing, for this was the way the world worked, and she might as well just get used to it, for it wasn't going to change.

At least he was smart enough not to say the words aloud.

"Can I ask you a favor?" she said, looking up from her invitations at him, and he seemed wary, but he nodded.

"Of course. I will grant it if it is in my power."

"Will you tell me if you and Gideon find anything in your search, or if you solve the riddle?"

He tilted his head at her, as though he could read her thoughts.

"As you will be conducting a search of your own, will you not?"

"I was going to do so from the start," she said with a shrug. "It would make more sense to do so together, but if Gideon is not going to allow it, then—"

"I will talk to him," Devon said. "I do not like the thought of you searching alone."

"Because trouble might find me?" She arched a brow, and he frowned.

"Cassandra—"

"I am teasing you," she said, reaching a hand out toward him, pitying him and all he had to put up with. "I know I am not the easiest woman to be around, truly I do. I argue and I do like to be in control, and I often feel slighted by the way that others – most especially men – act around me." Her voice softened then as she stared at him. "But I care for you, and I understand how you might feel. Gideon is right. I often find myself in troublesome situations. I am just not sure if it is because I am unlucky or because I don't back down when I should."

"You *are* rather stubborn," Devon said, but quickly proceeded with, "but that is something that I appreciate about you. It is not a reason to doubt yourself."

"Thank you," she said with a small smile.

"As for this riddle," he said, tapping a finger on his lips, "I know how frustrating it is becoming to have no leads and no results from searching. However, I believe we would be best served to solve the riddle rather than to continue to search all of Castleton. This estate is huge and we do not even know how small or big the treasure is. We could spend years searching and still not find anything."

"You have a point," she murmured. "So why did you humor me all of this time since we arrived?"

"Isn't it obvious?" he asked, and when he smiled at her, Cassandra wished his dimples were not quite so deep, for it made him rather difficult to resist. "Because I wanted to spend more time with you."

"Even when we first arrived?" she asked, feeling her brows rise along with her incredulity.

"Even more so then," he said. "For it was the one way that I knew you would allow me to be in your presence."

"You're very sweet."

"Like sugar."

She shook her head, then, laughing at him. "What will we do when all of our friends arrive?"

He shifted forward on the sofa, leaning down with his elbows upon his knees. "When you are ready, I will speak to Gideon about courting you," he said. "Although perhaps you are right and the best time for that is when we are not living under the same roof. For it would only bring about suspicion that we have been alone together – and we would never be allowed this freedom again."

"As we have right now?" she asked, her eyes flicking to the door, which he had left open, although no more than a crack.

"Just like right now," he said, and Cassandra took a chance, rising from the small desk where she had been writing to walk toward him.

"Perhaps I should just—"

"Cassandra?" The door flew open to reveal Gideon standing there. "Ah, Devon, there you are as well. I was looking for you."

Disappointment at the interruption filled her, but she continued walking back to the desk, as though she had already been on her way there.

"Gideon, it is good to see you. I was—actually, I was just about to tell Devon that I have heard back from our aunt."

"About the jewels?"

"Yes. She said she does have them in her possession – and that her mother gave them to her. So they are not the treasure we are looking for, unfortunately."

"I do not suppose she is interested in selling them for us?" Gideon asked, only half in jest, and Cassandra eyed him with a look.

"I know. We are not begging from our aunt. Is that all?"

"Not quite. I have the invitations prepared," she said, holding them out to Gideon. "Do you approve?"

"Of course," he said, before tilting his head toward the doorway. "And thank you. Shall we go?"

Devon nodded, although as he stood, he looked up and met Cassandra's eye, his gaze saying much more than his words ever could.

It was a promise. A promise that someday, Gideon wouldn't be interrupting them, but would understand why they were spending this time together – and that he would have no choice but to allow it.

She just wasn't sure when that day should be.

CHAPTER 20

*T*ime seemed to inch along over the next week. Devon wished that he could openly display his affection for Cassandra, as he was finding it difficult to spend meals with her, sit with her in the drawing room, pass her in the corridors, and have to pretend that he was entirely unaffected by her presence.

He had thought keeping their affections secret would allow them more unquestioned time together, but the truth was, it was nearly impossible to be alone, for every time they were in the same room together, it seemed as though her mother or Gideon found them. Today, the rest of their party was scheduled to arrive, and while it would seem that would make any potential opportunity completely disappear, Devon wondered if it would perhaps allow them to hide within the chaos.

He could but hope.

For he missed her – desperately. Even though she was there with him all the time, he longed to hold her, to touch her, to wrap his arms around her, to tell her how he was feeling about her.

It was damned irritating that he could think of almost nothing else, but his mind wasn't giving him any choice.

"It looks like the first carriage is arriving," Gideon said from beside him as they took afternoon tea together, along with Cassandra, who sat just out of reach, as always. "Who do you suppose it will be?"

"Hope and Faith," Cassandra said, looking out beyond. "They are closest, and that looks like their family crest upon the carriage."

"Will their mother have accompanied them?" Gideon asked, to which Cassandra nodded.

"I would assume so," she said. "Besides, she will be quite interested to see the current state of Castleton for herself."

Gideon cringed. "Mother will not be pleased."

"No," Cassandra said, shaking her head. "But we are not going to spend the rest of our lives in hiding because we are ashamed."

Devon knew she was likely referring to far more than just Castleton, but he couldn't help the swell of pride in his chest at her words. Her confidence was one of the things he admired the very most about her.

"I shall go welcome them," she said, standing, and when they rose with her, she lifted a hand. "Stay. I'm sure there will be many more carriages to greet in due time."

She was right, as the rest of the day was like a parade, with one guest after another arriving. Devon didn't miss the looks of concern on the faces of the servants, and when he saw the duchess greeting visitors in the foyer, she seemed nearly beside herself.

"All will be well, Mother," he heard Cassandra murmur to her. "We shall have a wonderful time, and everyone loves Castleton."

Devon hadn't been lying when he had said that Castleton held a certain charm. From the ruins to the gardens to the lake itself, the exterior held its own appeal that could not be denied. Even though the interior was falling apart, its character was held in the staid, dark brick, the arches over the doorways, the décor of the bedrooms. As much as it all likely should have been redone by now, it was like walking through history of various eras.

Of course, Devon wasn't entirely sure that a woman like Lady Embury would feel the same, but he hoped that she wouldn't voice any contrary opinions to the duchess, for he knew how insulted she would be.

As the gentlemen arrived, they began to congregate in the billiards room, although few of them actually played but rather had a drink and caught one another up on any recent occurrences.

The women, he assumed, were upstairs in a drawing room, although if he knew this particular group as well as he thought he did, they were not going to be gossiping and perfecting their needlework.

They were much more likely speaking of banned books and attempting to solve riddles.

Dinner was a rousing affair with the many voices, even as the duchess seemed rather on edge. The duke, however, was quite thrilled with the company around the table.

"Welcome all to Castleton," he said, his arms spread wide to greet them all. "It is lovely to have you all in my home again."

If Devon was correct, it seemed that the duke believed them to be men he had known in his youth, but no one commented upon it and rather seemed pleased to be so welcomed by the duke's good spirits. The food was as suspect as always, and many of the plates were returned to the kitchen untouched. Devon noticed Cassandra and Gideon exchange a glance, and he wished that he could assure them no one was judging them.

Although he was likely wrong in that. For even though all of their close friends would understand, the chaperones who had accompanied the young ladies were likely questioning the sense in coming here – and the duchess wondering why she had allowed it.

It was a slight relief when the ladies retired to the drawing room, for then the gentlemen were able to discuss the riddle.

First, however, Whitehall had something to say.

"Listen, Ashford, I know you want to find this treasure and restore your coffers to what they once were," he said, not mincing words. "But how long do you want to spend on this chase that could lead to absolutely nothing? It is striking more like a childish game and I think we had best be done with it. It is a waste of our time."

"Now, listen here—" Devon began, as quick to defend Gideon as he was his sister, but Gideon held up a hand.

"I can fight my own battles now," he said quietly to Devon, who nodded in understanding. "Whitehall, you might be entirely correct, and if so, I understand and appreciate your sentiments. But until we prove it to be an impossibility, how is this treasure hunt any worse than some of the other things we have done?"

They were all silent for a moment, Rowley snorting as he was obviously remembering a prank or two.

"Everything else we do is for the thrill," Whitehall continued to argue. "This is… it's a bore, to be honest. It is a manual labor search that none of us are particularly adept at. There are many other things I would far rather be doing."

"Such as?" Gideon asked, spreading out his hands in front of him.

"Such as wooing women. Rowing in races. Dressing up statues. Convincing Lord Peabrook that he has won an extravagant contest."

Devon couldn't help but smile. They had come up with some fairly creative ideas in the past.

"Just because we are solving this riddle does not mean that we cannot have a few games on the side," Ferrington said, his disposition as sunny as Whitehall's was cloudy. "Why not this? Let us have a wager for the time we are here. Whoever can come up with the most outlandish hoax will be the victor. In the meantime, if we are able to solve a couple of clues for Ashford, then all the better."

Gideon seemed somewhat uncertain about that, but when the other gentlemen began to nod in agreement, he sighed. "Very well. But nothing that will upset my mother or involve my family, understood?"

"Of course," they were all quick to agree.

He hadn't said anything about involving the other women, but Devon knew one thing was for certain – if he wanted to remain in Cassandra's good graces, neither she nor her friends could be the subject of their prank. He could only imagine what the rest of the men were going to come up with. Perhaps it would be best if he sit this one out entirely.

He hoped he didn't look guilty when he sat down next to her once they joined the ladies in the drawing room.

"I must admit that when I pushed the idea of this visit on my mother, I had forgotten about Lady Embury," Cassandra murmured in his ear later as she took a seat next to him on the sofa. He had known she was there without even seeing her, sensing her presence with a tingling up his spine.

"Your mother will charm them soon enough," he said, "and they shall forget all of the hardship that your family – and Castleton – has had to endure. Do not fret."

"I never fret."

Devon smiled, not answering, for he knew that to argue with her would just incense her all the more.

"Where are you beginning your search tomorrow?" he asked, turning to look at her.

"We have decided that continuing to search is not the best tactic."

"No?"

She shook her head. "We would be best to solve the riddle first."

"Do you have any ideas?"

"As a matter of fact—"

"Lord Covington, how wonderful to see you again."

Lady Madeline, who Devon recalled was Cassandra's closest friend and the only one who knew of their first tryst, sat down in between them.

"And you, Lady Madeline," he said, bowing his head toward her. "You look lovely, as always."

"Thank you," she said. "I trust that you and Cassandra have been getting on well in your time here alone?"

There was a glint to her eye, and he knew that she was suspicious of him – as she should be.

"We have been having a wonderful time, thank you."

"Good." She leaned toward him, lowering her voice so that only he could hear, although he noted that Cassandra was watching her closely. "If you hurt her again, I do not care who you are or how powerful you are, but I will never let you get away with it. Do you understand me?"

His eyes widened, but he nodded. "Understood, Lady Madeline," he said, trying to prevent the smile from forming on his lips, for he knew how serious she was and he had no wish to cause her to think he was mocking how much she cared for her friend.

"I am glad to hear it," she said, sitting back with some satisfaction. "Shall we toast to it?"

He eyed her drink as well as Cassandra's, wondering just what was within their glasses.

"I am always happy to toast with beautiful women," he said, earning him suspicious looks from both of them, and he couldn't help but laugh. "One day you will learn that I wish nothing but the best for you," he said, holding up his glass. "To solving riddles."

"To solving riddles," they said, and as they drank them back, he wanted nothing more than to make all of Cassandra's wishes come true.

CHAPTER 21

*C*assandra flew up into a sitting position in bed in the middle of that night, after waking with a start.

They had been speaking the entirety of the day about the riddle, and she had gone to sleep with the words still swimming around in her mind.

Something must have jarred itself loose in her subconscious, for a thought had come to her in her dreams, one that made so much sense now she felt silly that it hadn't previously occurred to her.

All she had to do was check the veracity of one fact – and then perhaps she had solved a piece of the riddle.

She should wait until morning, truly she should. Then she could enlist the help of Gideon, who would actually know just as much as she would regarding this particular conundrum, but she knew that she wouldn't be able to return to sleep until she had ascertained the truth for herself.

She flung her wrapper around her shoulders, tying the belt of the red silk tightly before tugging slippers onto her feet and padding toward her door. She opened it to make sure that no one was about in the hallway – she wouldn't want anyone to believe she had some secret nighttime assignation – and then continued down the carpeted corridor. The house was dark and silent but for the occasional creak. Cassandra, however, had no fear but instead was comforted by the familiarity of the house.

The library was near the front of the manor, and where she had left the riddle.

She pushed open the door, surprised to find a fire still burning in the grate.

"Is anyone here?" she called out, but only silence responded.

At first.

Then suddenly a figure materialized from the shadows of a corner and she had to stifle a scream at her surprise, until she recognized the stature of the body that was walking toward her.

"Devon?" she called out, placing a hand over her heart. "Why didn't you say anything? You scared me out of my wits!"

He smiled but lifted a hand and raised a finger to his lips before tilting his head toward the sofa. She tiptoed forward and saw her brother lying there, fast asleep outstretched on the cushions.

She had to stifle a laugh but leaned in toward Devon, lowering her voice as she placed her lips by his ear. "Should we put ink on his face for him to be discovered come morning?"

Devon chuckled lowly, but instead of answering linked his arm through hers and drew her away from the sitting area to a farther part of the library, which was cooler away from the fire but also quieter.

"What are you doing wandering the halls at this hour, dressed in such tempting clothing?"

Cassandra's lips quirked at that. This red silk wrapper

had always made her feel rather sensual, but she had never thought she would actually wear it for a man.

"I came for the riddle," she said, her excitement continuing to grow as she remembered just what had risen her from her bed. Devon had distracted her from her purpose tonight. "I had a thought."

"Did you now?"

"About the way the words are laid out," she clarified. "I think we have been reading it all wrong. What if it is not the words themselves that are leading us to the clue, but the words within it?"

Devon frowned at her. "I am not sure I understand. Can you clarify for the uneducated?"

She reached into the book sitting on the desk and pulled out the riddle, the paper crinkled from her folding it and refolding it over and again. She led Devon toward the small desk in the corner of the room and picked up the quill pen, dipping it in the ink before she began to make circles on the paper.

"What if it's not a riddle but a code?"

"A code?"

"Yes," she said, her excitement building. "I think it is actually telling us what we should be looking for in the rest of the document. You see here? I think it is a code of which words to look at."

She continued, circling the pattern as she had tried to describe to him. He leaned in, and a shiver of anticipation shook down her spine when his breath brushed across the back of her neck, his deep voice in her ear.

"I think you're on to something," he said, and she nodded.

"I believe we were correct in coming here to Castleton," she said. "It's in a building on the grounds."

"It's not referencing just any building, though," he murmured, his finger running over the paper, and she had to shake her head as all she could imagine now was his finger running over her body.

"A horse," she said, her voice just above a whisper. She looked up, her gaze meeting Devon's as they came to the same conclusion at the same time. She loved the spark that filled his eyes, even though finding such a treasure would make no difference to his own life. He loved the thrill of the chase as much as she did.

"The stables!" they said together, and Cassandra grinned wide. "I cannot wait to tell Gideon that we've solved it."

"You're giving me some credit, then?" he asked, before shaking his head. "You shouldn't. You solved this yourself. I was just here to watch."

He leaned in, then, framing her face between his hands. "You are something else, do you know that?"

"I believe I do," she said, "but it is still nice to hear it from your lips."

"You do know there is much more I can do with these lips."

"I am well aware," she said, her breaths coming quicker as he captured her mouth with his. He reached out and framed her hips with his hands, drawing her in closer toward him, his pelvis pressing against hers in a promise of what he had to offer her. Cassandra felt utterly wanton and loving it as she accepted him, not backing up but eagerly returning offering her body toward him.

"Perhaps we should go elsewhere," she murmured against his lips as she lifted her head for a moment, loathe as she was to tear herself away from the teasing and tempting of his tongue. "Gideon could wake up at any moment."

Devon blinked a couple of times. "Gideon. I had forgotten about him."

"*You* forgot about Gideon?" Cassandra said incredulously. "I can hardly believe that to be true."

"It is hard for me to think about anything or anyone else when you are around, luv," Devon said with a wicked grin that had Cassandra rolling her eyes at him, wondering how much of what he was saying was truth and how much was his usual charm that he made available to everyone.

"Should we go to the stables now?"

"It is the middle of the night!" he exclaimed. "We'll go first thing in the morning. I promise. We can rise before anyone else and greet the day with the horses and the grooms."

"You are not known to be an early riser."

"I can be when I have something exciting to look forward to," he said, tugging her even closer.

"Like a treasure?"

"If that is what you choose to call yourself."

He took her lips again, though the truth was, had he not, she would have initiated the kiss herself, for she didn't think she could take another moment without his lips against hers.

He was intoxicating, and she wasn't sure that she would ever get enough of him. Maybe it was time for them to speak to Gideon after all.

Devon had just worked his hand into her bodice, Cassandra arching up into him with a moan, when a voice cut through the passionate haze that had surrounded them.

"Unhand my sister!"

Cassandra gasped again, but for altogether different reasons, as Devon backed away abruptly, leaving her standing there with both her mouth and her bodice gaping open. At the very least, Devon had moved to stand in front of her, shielding her, but she wasn't sure if he had done so purposefully or if it was simply a fortunate position.

"This is not what it looks like," Devon said, and Cassandra frowned at his back. It was exactly what it looked like. She knew she had been the one to ask Devon not to speak to Gideon yet, and she realized belatedly that he had

been right – that a conversation would have been far prefer-
able than their current situation – but what were they to
do now?

"Gideon," she began, trying to step around Devon now
that she had put her clothing to rights, but Devon held an
arm out to keep her back.

"Cassandra and I were solving the mystery, that is all," he
said matter-of-factly.

"Was the mystery what was beneath her nightgown?"
Gideon said, the ire in his tone obvious. "Did you really think
you could take advantage of her just because she… well,
because she has been known for such liaisons?"

"Gideon!" Cassandra said, her fury at both her brother
and Devon growing with each word they spoke. "How can
you, of all people, say such a thing?"

"It's not like that," Devon said, holding out a placating
hand before Gideon could respond, and Cassandra waited
for him to defend her, to admit that, this entire time, it had
been him, and only him, that she had ever been found with –
but he just stammered his own defense of the two of them, as
though nothing had happened. "I would never—well,
Cassandra and I are friends, you know that—"

"Do I?" Gideon said, Cassandra's normally mild-
mannered brother was anything but mild now. "I always
thought that the two of you were at odds with one another,
and yet here you are, in my library – *as I slept on the sofa* –
cavorting with her."

"Gideon, I would never do anything to purposefully hurt
your family," Devon said, clearly more concerned with what
her brother would consider a betrayal than Cassandra's own
feelings. "Cassandra and I have been working on this riddle
together since you left, and we came to a similar conclusion
at once."

"You know what this means, do you not?" Gideon said,

his voice hard, and Devon stepped forward to try to placate him.

"It doesn't have to be like this," he said calmly, but Cassandra'd had enough of this. It was her past coming back to haunt her, this far too similar to the situation five years ago. Last time, Devon had run away. He might not be doing so now, but he was currently acting as much of a coward as he had then.

"Do not despair, Gideon, your friend has been faithful to you," she said, sweeping by Devon with a swish of her wrapper. "It was me – as it always is – acting the wanton and throwing myself at him."

"Of course you weren't," Devon said, shaking his head. "Why do we not sit down and speak—"

"I think enough has been said – or not said – already," Cassandra said, blinking away the tears that were threatening. "I am going to bed. Goodnight."

She stormed from the room, but when she entered the corridor, she stopped, standing next to the entrance. She was waiting for Devon to defend the two of them, to request her hand, to hear what he might have to say to her brother that might demonstrate that he truly cared, that this was all more than a liaison between the two of them, that she meant as much to him as he told her that she did, that she hadn't fabricated all of this within her own mind.

"Is what she said true?" Gideon said in a low voice. "Or was this all part of your elaborate scheme to win the contest?"

Contest?

Before Devon could respond, Gideon continued. "I told all of you not to include my family in your plots – especially my sister. We have our games, have our fun, but she is off limits. How could you not understand that? I know we said the wager was who could create the greatest scandal but this—"

"Gideon," Devon began, but Cassandra had heard enough. If all Devon had wanted was to win a contest, then congratulations, he had done so.

But in the process, he had lost whatever had been building between them.

If it had even been true to start with.

CHAPTER 22

"*I*t is not what you think," Devon said to his friend, who stood staring at him with glowering eyes, made more furious by the fire in the grate behind him that seemed to frame his head. That was not what most upset Devon, however. Instead, it was the betrayal lurking deep within Gideon's gaze.

"You were not compromising my sister to create a scandal and win our bet?" Gideon asked, each word clipped as he crossed his arms over his chest. "Brava, my lord, for it is the ultimate scheme."

"I *was* compromising her," Devon admitted. "But not purposefully. And it had nothing to do with the bet or a scandal. You should know I would never do such a thing. It has everything to do with the fact that... that I love her."

As he said the words, a warmth washed through his entire body, pooling within his chest where he supposed his heart resided. It hadn't been used often, he considered. He loved his family, yes, and he had a good many friends he was loyal to, but a woman? As he looked back on his past, however, he knew one thing was for certain. There had been no opportunity to love any other, for he had always loved Cassandra. He had just been too stubborn to realize it.

"You love her," Gideon repeated, obviously not believing a word of it. "Let me ask you this. Was this the first time that the two of you…"

He couldn't seem to finish his sentence and instead waved his hand in a circle, pointing to where he had discovered them.

"No," Devon admitted with a sigh, running a hand through his hair. "Gideon, I think this story requires a drink."

Gideon nodded tersely, leading the two of them over to the fire as he poured them each a brandy. Devon didn't think he could ever imbibe in the drink again without thinking of Cassandra.

"Well?" Gideon said, crossing one ankle across the other knee as he took a seat in one chair, gesturing to Devon to take the other. "I'm listening."

"I first compromised her five years ago."

Gideon's sole reaction was the blinking of his eyes.

"I do hope you are jesting," he finally said.

Devon shook his head. "I am not. It should never have happened, Gideon, I know that. Afterward… I tried to reach out to her, vowed to make it right, but she wanted nothing to do with me. She wouldn't even speak to me besides to tell me that she… well, that she was not with child and that she never wanted to see me again."

"Why would you not have come to me with this? I would have ensured that she married you."

"Yes, of course I knew that, but what kind of marriage would that be?" Devon asked, splaying his hands out between them. "You know Cassandra as well as anyone. If she were forced to do something, she would have been miserable. She would have hated me more than she already did and would have been equally as disgruntled with you. I didn't know about her being sent away. I would never have let that happen if I did."

Gideon was silent for a moment as he passed the drink from one hand to the other, his expression still wary, although he was, at least, listening. Devon also hadn't missed the flicker of guilt that had passed over Gideon's eyes when he had mentioned Cassandra's forced exodus to a place she had never belonged. "And now?"

"We have become... close since being here together. I wanted to tell you as soon as you returned, to ask for her hand, but she didn't want you to be suspicious of us, to know that we... well, that we went behind your back. I never meant to, Gideon, truly I didn't."

They were both silent for a moment, considering all of the repercussions this revelation would have on each of their lives – in every way.

"What are you asking me now?"

"I would like to ask if you would provide your permission for me to request her hand. I know I don't have the right to, and I do not want you to think it is because the two of us were caught. I would have asked years ago if I'd had any hope that she would willingly agree. Yet I still waited for her – I just wasn't sure if the right time would ever come."

"And you believe now is that time?'

"I now realize there *is* no right time."

"Except that now you have likely made acquiring her agreement all the more unlikely."

Devon chuckled without any humor. "I am well aware of that."

Gideon stared at him, the emotion in his eyes nearly impossible to decipher.

"I cannot say that I am pleased with how this has all come about," he said with a sigh, "but obviously after what I have witnessed and what you have told me, I cannot do anything but agree to your request for her hand. However, I will not force my sister, and she didn't seem particularly pleased with either of us. Which means that your chance of obtaining her agreement is likely going to be the most difficult aspect of all of this."

Devon sat back in his seat, as both relief at finally unburdening this secret as well as concern over what Cassandra's response might be, washed over him. He wanted nothing more than to chase after her, to tell her what she meant to him, to convince her to start a life with him.

But to do so now would make everything all the worse. He had to proceed in a way that would convince her of the truth – that this had all meant something to him, that he wanted to marry her because he loved her and couldn't imagine a life without her – and for no other reason.

It would have been far easier if she was a different woman.

But if she *was* anyone else, he would not love her as he did. So, he sat across from his friend, lowered all his defenses, and, for the first time in both of their lives, he asked for his help.

* * *

DEVON WOKE the next morning with an ache in both his chest and his head.

He knew the headache was likely from the bottle of brandy that he and Gideon had finished off the night before. They had spoken at great length about the past, finally free to share all that had occurred and all that Devon hoped for — although he wasn't sure that he would ever completely gain back Gideon's trust.

The ache in his chest was the concern about what

Cassandra was feeling this morning, what she might say to him after all that had occurred the previous night.

He had, unfortunately, allowed history to repeat itself.

Except this time, he knew better. This time, he was going to fix it and find the ending both he and Cassandra deserved. This time, he was going to finish this with the proposal he should have issued five years ago.

After a few more minutes of sleep and a cup of coffee in bed, Devon felt infinitely better, and when he finally descended the staircase, it was with a bounce in his step and a whistle on his lips. He had missed breakfast with most of the guests – including Cassandra – and he went in search of her, not surprised when he found her in the parlor with the other female guests.

Apparently, she had waited for him to visit the stables. That was a good sign.

But first, there was another matter of importance.

He took a breath as they all looked up at him in surprise when his frame filled the doorway.

* * *

"GOOD MORNING," Devon greeted the table, and Cassandra hated her traitorous heart for skipping a beat when she saw him. She noted her friends staring back and forth between her and Devon with uncertainty and an appropriate bit of malice for him, which was fair. She had shared all with them this morning. They had been equally shocked at both her past with the earl as well as the fact that what she thought had been a growing connection between them had, in fact, all been for a ridiculous wager.

Cassandra herself could hardly believe it. Here she had finally put her trust in him again, had believed that he could, perhaps, be the man for her, that her mind could accept what her body and heart were trying to tell her.

But it was all for naught. He was as devious as he had always been, looking out for himself and Gideon, while she was nothing but a pawn in his game.

What she hated most was how much it had affected her. After she had heard the truth last night, she had hurried back to her bedchamber, doing her utmost to keep her composure before anyone could see how distraught she truly was. She had fallen asleep with tears on her cheeks and pain in her heart, both of which had still been with her this morning.

"Lady Cassandra," Devon said, his hands behind his back in an unassuming pose, and her eyes narrowed at the fact he could think that he would trick her once more, "would you have a moment to speak with me?"

Her head snapped up to his.

"No, I would not."

His eyes widened, although she didn't care that he know how upset she was about last night. Damn him, standing there so completely unaffected, his handsome face in repose.

"I promise that I shall be brief," he tried again, and she was still shaking her head when Gideon filled the doorway behind him.

"Give the man a chance to explain, Cassandra," Gideon said with exasperation, and finally Cassandra realized there was but one way to end this. She brusquely pushed her chair away from the writing desk in front of her, cleared her throat, and issued an apology to her friends before she was brushing past the two men in the doorway with a flurry of skirts.

"I am *not* pleased with this," she muttered as she passed, noting Devon exchange a look with Gideon. Let the two of them attempt all they wanted. She was not going to break before them. Not this time.

Gideon led them into his study, hesitated for a moment as though wondering whether he should remain, but finally shook his head and retreated.

"I'll leave you to it, then, but I shall remain close," he said, his words an obvious warning that nothing untoward should occur again. He had nothing to worry about there. "Best of luck."

Cassandra scoffed as Devon thanked him. Cassandra leaned back against the desk, awaiting whatever charming words he had planned for her with her arms crossed.

"I do not appreciate being forced into this conversation," she began.

Devon lifted a brow as he took a chair in front of the desk, gesturing to the other for her. She paused for a moment before doing as he suggested, although not without a slight flounce as though to tell him she was doing so of her own will.

"You do realize that most women would be forced into marriage at this point," he said. "I hardly believe you should complain about a conversation with me, nor am I aware of why you are so displeased."

Her eyes widened. "*You do realize* that last night was a repetition of all that occurred five years ago."

"I can hardly agree with that," he said, shaking his head. "Five years ago, you were found alone after I left, only to face the repercussions yourself. I believe last night it was *I* who remained to face your brother."

"And just how did that conversation play out?"

"Cassandra, enough of this," he said, his annoyance obvious. "I am tired of the back and forth, of determining who is at fault and of both of us living in our past. What matters is the future, and I would like our future to be together. It is clear that neither of us will be happy with anyone but each other. No more secrets, no more uncertainty. I wish to marry you." He sank down on the floor in front of her. "Cassandra, will you be my wife?"

She said nothing for a moment as she stared down at him. Chills raced up and down her spine, her chest warming, and she hated that there was such a large part of her that wanted to say yes, that she could see a life with him, that she could picture days filled with laughter and friendship and everything she had ever wanted in a husband. Yet it would all be a lie. Because he didn't actually love her. Yes, he obviously desired her and perhaps they could forge something together, but she would know that it had all been based on misplaced loyalty to her brother and a desire to win a wager with his ridiculous thrill-seeking friends.

"No."

"I— Pardon me?"

"I said no," she said, her eyelids batting furiously up and down, as she struggled to keep her tears from falling once more. His face fell in apparent disappointment, but it was likely more irritation at her rejection than the heartbreak she would feel were he the one to deny her.

"Cassandra—"

"This was all a mistake," she said, annoyed by the crack in her voice as she stood and hurried to the door. She paused in front of it. "We were better off having never come back together again."

And with that, she rushed out of the room, leaving her heart behind.

CHAPTER 23

*D*evon wasn't sure how long he remained kneeling on the ground in front of the chair, but it was where Gideon found him when he entered following Cassandra's dramatic exit.

"It went as I thought it would, then, did it?"

"I don't understand," Devon said, turning his face up to his friend. "I thought that even if she didn't love me, that she at least *wanted* me. After five years, she never found another. Why?"

Gideon shrugged. "Her reputation was rather ruined."

"But still—"

Gideon placed a heavy hand on his shoulder for a moment. "I know. Come, have a drink," he said. "I'll try to talk to Cassandra."

"It won't help."

"Likely not. But perhaps we can come up with something to convince her."

"I don't want to coerce her," Devon said. "I want her to marry me because she loves me, because she cannot imagine a life without me."

"That cannot be forced," Gideon said quietly. "But I will do what I can to make her see reason."

Devon nodded, staring at the floor. "You will want to speak with her anyway. I believe she was close to solving the riddle last night. We *were* discussing it before… before."

"Very well," Gideon said and then sighed. "Well, we are to go fishing today. That should help take your mind off things."

Devon shook his head. "I shall remain behind."

"But—"

"I would be more of a liability than anything else at the moment," Devon said. "Go. Have a good time. I shall be here waiting afterward. Tomorrow, however, I should return to my own estate. I have remained here far too long as it is."

"You will leave now? Before we have solved the riddle?"

"It doesn't matter anymore," Devon said. "You will solve it without me. I hope I have helped you, but the truth is, my own interest came from spending time with Cassandra."

Gideon paused for a moment, seeming stalled in his own uncertainty. "Very well. But if you change your mind—"

"I know where you'll be."

Devon heaved a sigh as he rose to his feet in search of his chamber – he had some packing to do.

* * *

DEVON'S BAGS WERE PREPARED, but he had nowhere to go at the moment. He couldn't start his journey until tomorrow, but he had, at least, advised his valet and driver that they would depart in the morning.

He was sitting on a bench looking out over the ground's small lake when he felt a presence behind him, although he knew without turning that it wasn't Cassandra, for he could sense her whenever she neared.

"Lord Covington?" came a hesitant voice, and he turned to find Miss Hope Newfield standing there awaiting him.

"Miss Newfield," he said with a nod as he stood to greet her. "I am afraid that I am not very pleasant company at the moment."

"As it happens," she said, sitting down to join him on the bench, "I am not here for company."

"Oh?" he said in surprise, looking around for her sister or mother. He would never have assumed Lady Hope to be an opportunist looking to trap a man into marriage, but wouldn't that be the greatest of ironies, if it was to occur now with her? "What can I help you with?"

"I thought perhaps you would like to know just why Cassandra turned down your offer of marriage."

His head snapped up at that. "She told you of that?"

"She told us what occurred last night, and then a maid overheard your conversation in the study. She told some of the other maids, who told my lady's maid, who told me."

"I see," he murmured. Goodness, that had all happened in a manner of a few hours. Was nothing secret anymore?

"Cassandra loves you."

"I must disagree with that."

"I know it likely seems so because of her denial of you, but the truth is, she said no because she felt that she would only be hurt again."

"I never meant to hurt her the first time," he protested, "and I never would again. I didn't leave this time. I stayed, and I spoke to Gideon—"

"A conversation in which you discussed a wager of sorts?" she said, tilting her chin down and looking up at him with an expression that labelled him a fool without her saying anything.

"A wager? Cassandra had nothing to do with any wager —" He stopped as realization dawned on him. "Gideon asked me if this had to do with the bet. She must have heard. But I quickly assured him that it had nothing to do with that. That was just a flippant remark made by Lord Ferrington. I didn't even agree to it, and we were not allowed to use any of Gideon's family in our pursuit to win."

Lady Hope bit her lip. "From what Cassandra said, she failed to hear any of that besides the first part. Not only does she believe that you betrayed her once more in wanting to appease Gideon, but she believes she was used for a bet. I know many women would agree to marriage with you under any circumstance, my lord, but not Cassandra."

"Not Cassandra," he murmured, considering that was the very reason he loved her and no other.

"Cassandra wants to marry for love. She will have nothing but."

"I see," he said, unable to sit any longer, as he stood and began to pace back and forth along the shore. "I must convince her that my proposal of marriage was out of love and nothing else."

"My lord," Lady Hope asked, standing herself, crossing her hands in front of her and staring at him with what he was sure was forced courage, "*do* you love her?"

"I do," he said firmly. "With every part of me."

"Then tell her," she said softly but with equal firmness. "That is what she wants to hear. However, you must make her believe you."

"Very well," he said as an idea began to form. "But I am going to need a little help."

* * *

As SHE SULKED in the library, Cassandra closed her eyes when she heard footsteps down the corridor beyond, hoping that they would pass by and leave her in peace. She knew that her current situation was primarily of her own doing – although she did place a good deal of the blame on Devon as well – but she wanted this moment to feel sorry for herself without interruption.

Her hopes were dashed, however, when the door creaked open and Gideon appeared within its frame.

"You seem pleased to see me," he quipped, entering without invitation and sitting down across from her on the very sofa he had been sleeping upon the night before.

"I have a good idea of why you are here," she said, lifting her chin defiantly, "and I must tell you that you are wasting your time. I am not going to marry a man just so he may win a wager. I must say, Gideon, you have all gone too far this time."

"Cassandra, this has nothing to do with a wager."

"So you say," she said, swinging her legs down off the arm of the chair and onto the floor. "But besides that, I know that Devon is your closest friend and this probably all seems like it would work out perfectly to marry me off to him. You would not only then find me a husband but also keep your best friend close."

"Do you really think I would marry you off for such a reason?"

Cassandra paused, sighing softly.

"No. But I do not think you fully understand."

"Perhaps I don't," Gideon said with a shrug. "But I also do not believe you are being fair to Devon. I had my doubts as well, after I discovered... well, what was between the two of you. I cannot say I was pleased to learn of the past, either, but the truth is, Cassandra, all I want is for you to be happy. Both of you."

"Noted," she said with a nod. "Are you not supposed to be fishing?"

"I am," he said, standing now, obviously realizing that he wasn't going to get anywhere with her. "The men are waiting for me. I had wanted a word with you first."

"Have you said anything to Mother?"

"Of course not," he said, frowning as he shook his head. "It would only worry her."

"Thank you," she said, biting her lip, considering how her mother had reacted the last time she had been caught in such a situation. "Is Father going to accompany you today?"

"Yes, as a matter of fact," Gideon said. "He is having a rather lucid day, so Anderson said he would bring him along. It will be good for him."

"He will enjoy that," Cassandra said with a smile.

"As will I," Gideon replied as he walked toward the door, although not without looking back at her. "Devon is a good man, Cassandra. I know you have had your differences with him in the past, but he was there for me when no one else would have been. I cannot imagine my days at school without him, and I do believe he cares for you a great deal. Soften your heart toward him if you can."

That was the very problem, however. For if she were to do so, it would leave her heart vulnerable to be irreparably broken. But she wasn't going to speak to Gideon about that, so instead she just nodded in encouragement for him to leave to join his friends on the nearby river – especially as it would mean Devon was going along with him, providing her a reprieve of having to watch for him appearing around every corner.

"Catch some fish, Gideon," she said, to which he thanked her before continuing on his way.

Cassandra leaned her head back against the sofa and closed her eyes. She had heard from her maid that Devon was preparing to leave tomorrow, a fact which brought her both comfort and sorrow. For as much as she yearned to see him again, for his touch and his presence, the sooner he was cut from her life, the better.

It was the only way she would ever be able to move on.

CHAPTER 24

*W*hen the next day dawned with no sign of Devon, Cassandra couldn't quite bring herself to ask anyone if he had, in fact, departed, although she couldn't think of any other explanation for his absence. She hated that she couldn't deny her longing to see him, and the hope that perhaps there had been more to his proposal, that he would prove her wrong by convincing her that he cared for her more than his ridiculous wager or because he felt he owed her brother for compromising her.

But it was as though the past was reoccurring – except this time, there would be no sending her away to learn how to better conduct herself. Perhaps she was just soiled goods, she thought morosely as she stared out the window. She knew that it wasn't completely uncommon for women to ruin their reputations, but she was likely one of the few ladies of her status who refused to do what was expected and marry the man who had so ruined her.

She had forced a smile to her face for breakfast, while she sensed a strangeness in the air, as though she was being watched – but every time she lifted her face, the others around the table quickly returned their gazes to their plates in front of them.

As soon as breakfast was over, Hope stood and clasped her hands in front of her.

"Shall we perhaps make for the parlor?" she asked, and Cassandra furrowed her brow. It wasn't like Hope to plan anything for the rest of them.

"I don't see why not," she said. "As it happens, I have an idea about the riddle I would like to share."

It should be something she was excited about, but it seemed she had lost all of her vigor for it now that she didn't have Devon to help her with it. She would tell Gideon all she had found, she decided, and then he could pursue it.

"Wonderful," Hope beamed, and Cassandra couldn't help but smile back. Hope was always a beacon of sunshine, and it was hard to not respond to her optimism about everything in life. She stole a glance at Madeline, not surprised to see that she seemed equally as skeptical as Cassandra did, but they made their way to the parlor without comment.

Once they had taken their seats, Hope sprang to her feet, her eyes bright as she gripped a sheath of papers in her hand.

"I have a story."

"Oh?" Cassandra said, surprised. "Where did you find it?"

"It is a story for you alone, Cassandra," she said, ignoring her question as she crossed the room and set the papers in her hands. Cassandra couldn't help her curiosity as she flipped through the pages, finding about five pages of hand-writing within. She looked up at her friends, who were watching her carefully.

"There are not copies for everyone?"

"No," Hope said. "Just for you." She looked to the rest of the women. "Perhaps we can read our own novels while you learn more of what awaits you."

"Very well," Cassandra said slowly, unable to help her

suspicion. Something was clearly amiss, but she supposed the only way to find out was to read. Perhaps it had something to do with the riddle. But why would Hope not have come to her immediately if she had discovered an answer?

"I can hear you thinking from across the room," Madeline said impatiently. "Just read."

"Very well," Cassandra grumbled as she set the pages down upon her lap and allowed her eyes to run over the heavy script.

Five years ago, our hero and heroine were at a house party, it began.

It just took a few lines to realize that the story written upon the pages was not just any story. It was *her* story. Hers and Devon's.

"Hope," Cassandra said imploringly, lifting her head, her eyes boring into her friend, but Hope simply shook her head.

"Keep reading," Hope said, her voice more insistent than Cassandra had ever heard it before. With the instruction coming from her most mild-mannered friend, she didn't seem to have a choice but to continue.

She knew the story well, and yet she couldn't help the quickening of her heart as her eyes skimmed the words in her need to know what was coming next. For the details included on the pages were those that only two people knew – her and Devon.

Had he written this? But why?

She forgot all of her questions, however, as she continued to peruse the page, needing to know how he would have this end.

She looked up at her friends, who were pretending to read but were quite obviously watching for her reaction to the story.

"You do know that I don't appreciate unhappy endings,"

she muttered, not missing the smiles they were trying to hide.

"Just read," Faith said with an exasperated sigh, and Cassandra tilted her head back down to finish the story. It told of what had happened five years ago – to her, and to the man who had left her, who had always regretted it, and had wanted nothing more than to apologize – and to make her his wife. Her pulse quickened at that, as Devon had told her what his intentions had been, and yet it seemed more real when it was written down in front of her. He had truly wished to marry her, all of this time?

All that had been holding him back, it seemed, was his belief that she wanted nothing to do with him – which made sense, considering that she had refused to talk to him, would not receive his messages or entertain any invitation to meet.

Her eyes began to smart, and she had to blink back the tears that threatened. So much time wasted, a lifetime that could have been...

The story continued to their time together here at Castleton, their search for the treasure, and what it had all led to – them being caught again in the library, and her refusal of his proposal, because she believed that it was nothing more than a ruse in order to win a wager with his friends.

The story finished with a sentence that echoed her own thoughts – of the tragic loss both of them had experienced in never knowing what true happiness could be, due to their own stubbornness and inability to tell one another their sincere feeling. There was no blinking back tears now as they rolled freely down her face, and as much as Casandra had no wish for any of her friends to realize how she was truly feeling, she looked up without shame.

"But why—" she began, only for her words to end on a gasp.

For as she had become caught up in the story, her friends had vanished, silently stepping out of the door.

But she wasn't alone.

Instead, a large frame stood in the doorway, light from the windows beyond shining behind him.

"Devon," she whispered, coming to her feet, uncertain of what to say, how to feel, what he wanted from her anymore. She lifted the pages toward him. "Did you write this?"

"I did."

"I hate tragic endings."

"I know," he said, one side of lips quirking upward. "So do I."

"Then why—"

He brought the hand that had been behind his back in front of him. "I have an alternate ending."

It was one sheet of paper, with just a few lines written upon it. Cassandra reached her hand out toward it, annoyed to find that her arm was shaking, but Devon didn't comment upon it. She took the paper from him wordlessly, looking down at it, blinking the sheen of tears away from her eyes so that she was able to read.

Fortunately, the hero soon realized his folly and was honest with the heroine. She finally overcame her own stubbornness and believed in his words. For he loved her, with all of his heart, and promised to love her forever. She admitted what was in her own heart, accepted his proposal, married him, and they both lived happily ever after.

She knew her mouth was gaping open as she looked up at him. "Devon—"

"Cassandra," he said, stepping forward and taking her hands within his, squeezing with the urgency of his words as he looked down at her. "I truly do love you, with all that I am. Our past has been filled with misunderstandings and miscommunication and unfortunate timing and decisions on both of our parts. Perhaps, now, instead of regretting the past, we learn from it and move forward together. For there is one important thing I will take from all that has happened between us – that I will never love another, and that you are more important to me than anyone or anything else."

"Even Gideon?" she asked with a wobbly smile.

"Even Gideon," he answered with a grin himself.

She stepped even closer toward him, closing the small gap that still existed between them.

"I've never been able to resist a happy ending," she said, tilting her face up toward him. "And, despite my very best efforts, I've never been able to resist you. I think it's time that I stop trying. For I love you too, Devon, with every part of me."

His grin spread even wider then as he looked down at her, released her hands, and then framed them around her face and brought her to him for a kiss that was more than a kiss – it was a declaration that she belonged to him, as he did to her, and a promise that they would have one another for the rest of their lives.

They finally broke away from one another when they heard a throat clearing behind them, but they kept their eyes on each other instead of turning to Gideon, who radiated both approval and disapproval at the same time.

"I've always been a sucker for a happy ending," Cassandra said, humor in her voice, and Devon laughed.

"How very fortunate for me."

Gideon apparently didn't appreciate being ignored any longer by his best friend and his sister, for he now stepped into the room, close enough that they had no choice but to acknowledge his presence.

"I think that is quite enough of that," he said. "I have allowed the two of you to be alone long enough."

"But Gideon," Cassandra said with an eye roll, "Devon and I—"

"Are to be married," Gideon interrupted. "As far as I am concerned, nothing else untoward has occurred. Now, we best go speak to Mother, of course, and then we have more business to discuss."

"Business?" Cassandra asked, furrowing her brow, and Gideon winked.

"We have a riddle to solve," he said, looking from her to Devon and back again. "What do you say we do it together?"

"I say," Cassandra said, placing her hands on her hips, "it is about time. Now, where is everyone?"

"Right here," Madeline said, appearing around the doorway. "We didn't go far."

"Were you spying on me?" Cassandra demanded, but without malice. For she didn't overly care, as she would have shared all with her friends anyway.

"We were," Percy confirmed. "And we are very happy for you. For both of you, Cassandra, my lord."

Cassandra left the room to seek out Hope, who wore an expression more coy than Cassandra had ever seen upon her before.

"That was quite the scheme," she said with admiration, causing Hope's cheeks to flush.

"I am just happy all worked out," Hope said.

"Which it did, better than I could have ever wished for," Cassandra said before looking around at the rest of them. "Now, what do you say we go solve this riddle?"

CHAPTER 25

*"A*re you sure about this?" Gideon asked as the ten of them filled the stables. They had been met by concerned stable hands who'd thought they had missed preparing the horses for the lot of them, but they had quickly assured them that they were there not to ride but to visit the horses.

Their confusion was evident; however, Gideon had relieved them of their duties for the remainder of the afternoon, leaving the stables empty for them to search.

"I'm not entirely certain, no," Cassandra admitted now, reaching into her pocket and pulling out the riddle. She held it out before her, reading the words she had committed to memory some time ago through the dusty light in front of her. "But once I determined that it was a code, it was easy to decipher. Whoever created it did not make it overly complex. We were so caught up in the riddle we didn't realize that it could be something else entirely."

"And what did you determine the code read?"

"You will find what you seek in this place where creatures never lay but always sleep."

Devon rubbed his chin. "I wonder if that is a stall, then."

"May I see it?" Whitehall asked, stepping forward, surprising them all. He hadn't seemed overly interested in the riddle before.

He noticed their surprise. "I have some experience with codes."

"How so?" Devon asked, for the viscount had never portrayed such experience before.

"It doesn't matter," Whitehall muttered. "Just give me the paper."

Cassandra passed it over, and Whitehall held it in his hand as he paced a few steps forward and then a few steps backward, muttering to himself as he did.

"It's in the last stall on the right."

They all stared at him.

"How did you know that?" Cassandra demanded. "It wasn't part of the code."

"There is another code embedded in it," Whitehall said. "One much more difficult to decipher."

"But—"

"Leave Whitehall be, Cassandra," Gideon said gently. "We can question him later. Let's search now."

She nodded, although Devon nearly laughed aloud at the suspicion she eyed Whitehall with. He knew better than to allow his mirth to show, however, and instead he took her arm as they walked toward the back of the stable.

"Hello there, old girl," Gideon said, stepping forward and rubbing the nose of the horse within. Devon knew she had been with the family for years, and while she was too old now to do much more than graze in the pasture, Gideon loved her and the rest of the horses far too much to let her go. The man loved his animals more than he did most humans. "What have you been hiding in here?"

The horse whinnied as though in answer to them, and

Devon started when he could have sworn the horse jerked her head to the back corner.

"Where could it be?" Cassandra asked, as she, Gideon, and Devon stepped into the stall, the rest of them waiting outside as they all couldn't fit without spooking the horse. "It is not as though there would be some treasure sitting out here in the open."

"It would only be in a wall or the floor," Devon said, rubbing his chin as he looked around them. "We best get to searching."

Gideon tried to convince Cassandra to remain outside the stall to allow room for another man to come into search, but she quickly quelled his suggestion with a look. They did, however, move the mare, Annabelle, to another stall. They ran their hands down the walls, trying to find any secret compartments, while Gideon and Devon found shovels to scrape the straw away from the floor to determine if anything was buried beneath.

Devon didn't see anything that gave away the location – instead it was the sound his shovel made when he brought it back to the floor.

"Cassandra?" he said, his voice low in a whisper, wanting to speak to her about it before anyone else. "Does this sound hollow to you?"

She joined him as he tapped his shovel on the floor, before she bent down in the straw, obviously uncaring that her skirts would be completely soiled after this.

"I'll do it," he said, but she waved him away, running her hands along the wooden floor, until she looked up at him with an excited grin.

"It does – and there is something here!"

That captured the attention of everyone, and soon they were all leaning over her as she found the nearly imperceptible seam in the floor, digging her nails into it until it finally cracked open and she was able to lift it up.

Devon realized he was holding his breath until he heard Cassandra's gasp, and then he couldn't help but kneel beside her, joining her on the floor as she revealed a dark, square compartment below.

She reached her hands in and pulled out a dirty velvet bag wrapped around something large and heavy before setting it beside her.

"What do you suppose it could be?" she asked, looking from Devon to Gideon and then up to the rest of them. "Coins? Jewels?"

"Should we take a bet first?" Devon asked, half jesting until Cassandra frowned at him.

"Could you seriously wait that long to open it?"

"I could, but I know you would be far too impatient."

"In that, you are correct."

She reverently brushed away loose straw and loosened the drawstring around the top of the bag before slipping her hands within, her eyes widening and meeting Devon's before she drew out the treasure.

They all stared in shock at the old dusty book that sat in front of them.

"That's it?" Whitehall said incredulously. "All of this for a book?"

Cassandra ignored him as she opened up the first page, and Devon waited with a quickly beating heart as surely there must be more to it. Could the book be hollow? Or was it some priceless manuscript hidden within an old, dilapidated cover?

But all that was within was a few images and text. Text that belonged to the book.

"What the bloody hell is this?" Gideon asked, causing

them to all stare at him in shock, for Gideon never, ever swore, no matter what company he was keeping.

Cassandra cleared her throat.

"It appears to be a book."

"I can see that," he said, rubbing his fingers against his forehead. "And just what are we supposed to do with a book?"

"I have no idea," Cassandra said, holding it out to him. "Perhaps there is more to it. Why do we not take it inside and look further into it?"

"There could be something hidden within the pages," Devon suggested.

"It could hardly be anything of value," Gideon muttered, and Devon saw the despair enter his eyes as he realized that his friend had been placing more hope upon this than he had even guessed.

"There is only one way to find out," Hope said from outside the stall with her usual bright optimism, and Devon met Gideon's eyes and nodded to him, silently telling him that there was nothing else they could do at this point.

Devon held out a hand to help Cassandra to her feet, and she clutched the velvet bag as Devon bent and set the floor and the straw to rights before Rowley led Annabelle back into her stall.

"Well, thank you, Belle," Gideon said, running his hand down her flank one more time. "I wish you'd had something else for me, but this will have to do."

Their party was practically silent as they returned to the house, stopping briefly for Gideon to find the butler and ask him to tell the stable hands they could return to their duties.

They all gathered in the drawing room as Gideon placed the book on the table amidst them all, and they sat staring at it as though it would suddenly gain magic and open to reveal a spell.

"Oh, there you all are!" They started when the duchess appeared in the doorway. Devon had nearly forgotten that she was in residence, although she spent most of her time upstairs with her husband. The chaperones had been keeping to themselves for the most part. "Are you all enjoying yourselves?"

"We are, Mother, thank you," Gideon said, and Devon didn't miss her eyes finish upon him with a wide smile. Apparently, the news of his engagement to Cassandra had made his way to her.

"Good," she said, clasping her hands together, her eyes flitting back and forth as though she was aware of the tension that filled the room, but had far too much breeding to address it. "Tonight we will have a celebratory dinner on the engagement. I know your family should be in attendance, Lord Covington, but we shall have another with them. I can hardly believe that my Cassandra will be married."

Her smile widened as her expression seemed filled with relief more than excitement, causing Cassandra's own smile to appear somewhat pained, and Devon decided that it was up to him to ensure that was put to rights.

"Thank you, Mother, that sounds lovely," Cassandra said, and it was then that the duchess' eyes fell upon the book on the table.

"What is this?" she asked, coming closer, picking it up.

"It is a book that we found," Gideon said, standing and coming behind her, holding out a hand. "We are… playing a game with it."

"A game?" This came from the doorway, as the duke now filled it. "I always enjoy a good game."

He entered the room with a smile for them all as he came over to his wife.

"What's this now?"

"A book, Father," Gideon said, his eyes landing upon the

duke as he was obviously trying to ascertain whether he remembered his true identity today.

"Ah, I recognize this story," he said. "An interesting one."

"You recognize it?" Gideon asked.

"Of course," the duke frowned. "It looks just like Newfeld's book."

"Our father's?" Faith said, exchanging a look with Hope. "I've never seen one like it before. Is it the same book?"

The duke took the book from his wife and turned it over. "It could be, or at least his is similar but does not appear to be the same. His mother held it in such high regard and kept it hidden. Which, naturally, caused us to want to see it all the more." He chuckled. "We looked that book over from cover to back and never could find anything special about it."

"I see," Gideon murmured, even though the explanation only made it all the more confusing.

"Wait," Cassandra said, and they all turned to her, finding her hand deep inside the bag. "There's something else within."

She pulled out an old, delicate, folded paper.

"It was within the lining of the bag," she said reverently, as she broke the seal and opened the page as they all waited, with nary a sound filling the room. "It appears to be a letter," she said. "A very short one with no apparent meaning."

"*Greetings, my dear friend! It was such a pleasure to see you again. There is nothing new to report. I look forward to spending some time with you when I come to town this summer. Until then, cordially yours, friend.*"

She looked up at them all. "There is a date at the bottom. I don't understand."

"I do," Whitehall said, surprising them all. "But this is not something we can solve today."

CHAPTER 26

"*A*s thrilled as I am about our engagement, I would really like to solve this mystery before we celebrate," Cassandra said, tapping her hand against her drink.

After Whitehall's revelation, they had prepared for the dinner that the duchess had arranged. While there was still an edge to the atmosphere, especially from Gideon who had finally accepted that there was no treasure immediately awaiting him to set his finances to rights, it had been an entertaining dinner with all ten of them plus their chaperones present.

Now that the men had joined them in the drawing room, Cassandra couldn't help but be drawn to Devon's side. It was hard to believe that, against all odds, they had found one another and overcome their past to plan a future together – one that Cassandra hoped would begin sooner rather than later.

As tired as she was – and as hopeful that she could perhaps find some time alone with Devon – they waited long enough that their parents and chaperones finally retired, leaving the rest of them the time they needed to discuss what their next steps might be.

"Well, Whitehall?" Devon said as they all stared at the surly viscount who did not seem to particularly welcome all of the attention suddenly directed his way. "Do you have a plan?"

Whitehall sighed in seeming resignation of his current position as he leaned forward and placed his drink on the table, interlacing his fingers together.

"I cannot say anything for certain until I see the other book in the set, but I am assuming, along with the note that was found with your book, that there will be a code present between the two. A book cipher. We will know when we compare one book to the other in order to determine if they would result in the same message and therefore break the code on the page. What appears to be an innocuous couple of lines could be something of much more importance."

Cassandra blinked in surprise as she realized that was likely the most she had ever heard the viscount speak at one time. His words had been clipped and short, but each one obviously carefully used to describe exactly what he meant to say.

"And this clue could lead us to the treasure?"

He lifted a brow as he stared at her with a look that made it clear he was not impressed by her question.

"I proposed a problem to solve the code, not to tell you what is in it."

"Now see here—" Devon began, but Cassandra placed a hand on his arm and a smile on her face.

"Thank you, Lord Whitehall," she said, for it would do no good to raise the man's ire. She looked around at the rest of them. "What do you say now?" she asked. "Should we move this party to Newfield Manor?"

206

Faith snorted. "I hardly think my mother would welcome a sudden influx of house guests with no warning."

"Are you certain?" Hope asked, her voice soft. "Do you not think she would be thrilled by the fact we would prefer to retire there than remain at Castleton?"

"Oh dear," Cassandra said. "I never thought of that. My mother would likely find it quite the insult, particularly because she already feels Castleton to be inferior to what it should be."

"I am loathe to suggest this, as I am as invested in this outcome as any other," Devon said, his voice low and warm at her shoulder, sending a most welcome trickle down her spine, "but I have been away from my own estate for far too long, especially now that I will be returning to share the news that a bride will accompany me."

He bestowed a smile on Cassandra at that.

"Would it be terrible to suggest that we take this up at a later date this summer?"

Everyone began to murmur among one another, but Cassandra alone seemed to note the trouble present on Gideon's face. Her heart went out to her brother, for she knew, despite what he said, that he had put considerable faith in finding the treasure to restore the fortune that they had lost.

"It will not be a long wait, Gideon," she said with forced optimism. "Just enough so that we are able to make a better plan."

They were all silent for a moment as they considered it, until Lord Whitehall unexpectedly spoke again.

"I have a suggestion," he said, and they all waited to see just what he might propose. "My mother is close friends with Lady Embury. Perhaps I could suggest a visit to Newfield Manor. There, I can begin to look at the two books and the clue, if you might permit me to borrow your copy, Ashford."

"Of course," Gideon said, his brows rising in surprise. "But do you have time to do so?"

The viscount shrugged. "My property isn't far. I will return, convince my mother to organize the visit, and then I should be able to attend." He turned to Hope and Faith. "Do you think it could be arranged?"

Hope's mouth had dropped open in surprise, and she blinked a couple of times as though uncertain of what to say, but Faith nodded.

"Of course," she said succinctly, and Cassandra supposed that it could work. Faith and Lord Whitehall were both efficient, if rather pessimistic people – she was sure they could see it through until they could all gather once more. "I shall speak to Mother on the morrow."

"There is one thing to note," Devon interjected. "You must be careful. We do not know with any certainty, but there is a chance that we were in some danger."

He told the story as briefly as possible, even as Gideon frowned at him.

"It was likely a hunter who mistook you for an animal, but of course, it never hurts to take extra care," Gideon said, standing and raising his glass. "Now, before we retire, one more toast to the happy couple."

They all smiled, raised their glasses, and clinked them together. As Cassandra met Devon's eye, she knew that, despite the lack of treasure and their inability to find what they had been looking for, she had discovered what truly mattered – this man before her, who had always been the other half of her heart.

* * *

THE DAY HAD BEEN one to remember – as successful as it could have been, and one full of celebration. But still, Devon lay in his bed, staring at the ceiling, wondering if sleep would ever come.

Which was why, when he heard the creak on the other side of his wall, he was instantly on edge – until his door opened a crack, and at the very first glimpse of the kid slipper that entered, his smile widened until he was fully grinning at the woman who slipped in through the door as though she was evading someone following her.

And perhaps she was.

"I don't believe you are supposed to be here, my lady," he said, laughter in his voice, and she let out a slight peep as she jumped, her hand coming to rest on her heart.

"You're not supposed to be awake," she said, before looking around, and then back at him, her gaze suddenly focused and direct, "however, this is exactly where I am supposed to be."

She took a few steps before diving onto the bed next to him, and he wrapped his arms around her and brought her closer.

"On that," he said, bringing his nose to touch hers, "I am in complete agreement."

"The thing is," she said, running her fingers over the side of his face, down his cheekbones to his lips, "we started something the other night, something that should have been finished in an entirely different way than it was. I know we will be together soon, but I am not an overly patient woman."

"You don't say."

"Perhaps," she said, her voice lowering to a whisper, her breath soft against his open collar, "we should return to where we were?"

She laced her fingers into his before lifting them and bringing them to the opening of her wrapper, taking their entwined hands and covering her breast with them.

ELLIE ST. CLAIR

"I think this is where we were," she said, before leaning in and placing her lips against his.

"Not quite," he couldn't help but argue as his lips quirked upward. "I believe I had discovered bare flesh."

He slid his hand across her wrapper, slipping it off her shoulders before her nightrail was up over her head, banished across the room as his fingers found her nipples and began to caress them while he kissed her again. Devon had to restrain himself from wanting too much too fast, as he did all he could to slow down, savour this – savour her – and take his time.

She pulled back for a moment, her eyes exploring his face before coming to rest on his mouth.

"For a man without much experience, you are awfully good at this," she murmured, and he changed his expression to appear affronted.

"Are you suggesting that I lied to you?"

"Not at all," she said, grinning wickedly. "It is that I believe I bring out the best in you."

"Perhaps," he said, tapping a finger against his chin to appear to be pondering her words. "Or perhaps it is that we are meant to be, that this is what we are supposed to be doing with one another."

"Perhaps you are right," she said softly, and he leaned in then and kissed her jaw, her neck, her collarbone, working his way down until she reached up and cupped his chin in her hand.

"Devon?"

"Yes, love?"

"You have far too many clothes on."

He gave her one quick kiss on the breast before he straightened and removed what remained of his clothing – his linen shirt and his breeches, until he was as bare as she was – just as he liked it.

He crawled on top of her, unable to help the predatory growl that escaped from his lips until he was hovering over her, kissing her on the lips, between her breasts, down her belly, then at her waist. She gasped and her hips arched up toward him.

"Devon—"

"I love you," he said, silencing her, as his strong hands gently spread apart her thighs, and his tongue brushed against her seam.

"Devon," she said again, but this time she said his name in supplication, as he began to move his tongue faster against her, hoping she was enjoying it – although by the way she moved against him and threaded her fingers into his hair, it seemed he had nothing to fear.

He slid two fingers inside of her, stroking her until she said his name loudly enough that he worried she would wake the house, and he decided that there was only one way to silence her.

He slid back up her body, pressing a finger and then his lips against hers as he positioned himself at her entrance, waiting for her to move against him in acceptance, and, when she did, found home.

"I love you," she said against his lips, and he answered her by moving back and forward again.

He leaned back to look at her while he was still buried within her.

"I don't deserve you, I know that," he said, reaching out and brushing her hair away from her face. "But I promise I will spend my life making sure you know you are the most loved woman there ever was."

"We deserve each other, Devon," she said with a languid smile. "It just took us awhile to realize it."

At that, he began to move against her, and her smile fell as she tilted her head back and met him stroke for stroke. As

Devon couldn't help but go faster with her, he promised himself that next time he would draw this out and make love to her slowly.

And the good news was, they had an entire lifetime to do just that.

EPILOGUE

Most of the young women Cassandra knew had dreamed of the day they would wed.

So had Cassandra – but her dreams had been closer to nightmares as she had always feared just who she would marry, what the man might want from her, and how she could ever remain the woman she wanted to be.

She had never thought that she might marry for love.

Here she was, the day after her engagement. Today they were having one final farewell luncheon before her friends would be on their way to their own homes. She looked across the room at Devon, standing so handsomely at the other end of the room, having his friends laughing at some story he was telling.

"Cassandra."

She turned to find her brother beside her, hands clasped behind his back, his expression contrite.

"What's wrong?" she asked Gideon, and he opened his mouth and then closed it a couple of times.

"I realize the timing is not ideal but before you begin the next stage of your life, I needed to speak to you."

"Now?" Cassandra asked, looking around the room, past the friends and family who had gathered, at Devon and back again.

"Yes. I must apologize. Close the door to the past, as it were."

"Whatever for?"

"For not stopping the family from sending you away. I should have spoken up for you, should have ensured that we stood by you, no matter what it meant for our family's reputation."

"Gideon." Cassandra reached out and placed one of her silk-clad hands on his sleeve. "It's finished. I understand."

"But—"

"You were hardly old enough yourself to stand up for what you believed in. I know that things would be different now. Neither of us are the people we were five years ago, which is a good thing."

"And as for Devon—"

"We have also — obviously — come to an understanding," Cassandra said, a smile playing on her lips. She appreciated what Gideon was doing, truly she did, but she had also made her peace. "You are right in that it is time for us to move on. We have learned from the past, and if nothing else, we will remember those lessons when it comes time for us to parent our own children."

"That we will," he said, his jaw still set stoically. "Thank you, Cassandra."

"Of course."

He nodded, his jaw ticking, and she realized how much this had been weighing on him. She reached out and squeezed his hand as their parents walked up to join them. They had been uncertain about Cassandra's father's involvement today, but this morning, by all miracles, not only was he in good spirits but he also seemed to be entirely aware that Cassandra was his daughter and not his sister.

"Cassandra, you look beautiful," her mother said, her hands clasped in front of her while her father nodded.

"You are certain of marrying this man?" he asked her, and Cassandra's heart warmed at what a good man her father truly was.

"Absolutely."

"Well, then," he said, "how long are we waiting for?"

"Not long," Cassandra said, sending her wide grin across the room to where her future awaited. "Not long at all."

* * *

"I AM LOOKING FORWARD to introducing you to my family," Devon said, having found Cassandra from across the room. "I'm sure they will be pleased that I have found a woman who can put up with me."

"Some might say that I am also something of a handful," Cassandra said with a cheeky wink at Devon that had his heart fluttering and his desire stirring to life, although he closed his eyes and made himself think of something else entirely, being that this room and the one connected were full of his entire family.

"Nothing I can't handle," he said, until he heard a throat clearing in his ear and he turned to find Whitehall standing there.

"Are you enjoying yourself?" Devon asked the man who he wouldn't entirely consider a friend but who seemed to be growing on him regardless.

"I suppose so," the viscount said with a shrug as though it didn't matter one way or another. "I must speak with you."

"Very well," he said, stepping away from the small group

they were speaking to so that they could have some privacy. "What is it?"

"It's about the book," he said, looking from one side to the other as though suspicious they might be overheard.

"What of it?"

"It doesn't make much sense to me that Lord Embury would be in possession of it."

"What are you saying?" Devon asked, leaning in closer, curious despite himself.

"I am saying," he said, his eyes hardening, "that I have some questions over his motivations."

Devon blinked as he stood straight, surprised by White-hall's suspicions, but winced when he saw just who was standing behind Whitehall. He tried to motion to his friend to stop talking, but the man didn't seem to understand his gestures.

"Lord Embury could be a thief. And while I will go and review the book, I will make sure that it is returned to where it belongs."

"What did you say about my father?" the normally mild-mannered Hope Newfield stepped forward, eyes blazing, and Devon couldn't help but take a step backward. This was his wedding day, and his single wish was to enjoy it. He locked eyes with Cassandra, who, despite being across the room, seemed to understand that something was amiss. He gave a nearly imperceptible shake of his head, telling her not to come near.

For this was someone else's problem now. And it was certainly going to make Whitehall's stay at Newfield Manor an interesting one.

And as he backed away, allowing Miss Newfield and Whitehall to figure this out for themselves, he focused on the woman who meant everything, the woman who had awakened his heart all of those years ago, and had never left it, despite how much he thought it was fast asleep.

He had solved the puzzle that mattered the most – how to find his missing piece. She was standing right in front of him, and he was never going to let her go again.

THE END

* * *

DEAR READER,

I hope you have enjoyed the first book of the Reckless Rogues! Wondering where the next clue leads to? You can follow the treasure trail and discover what comes next in The Viscount's Code, a grumpy vs sunshine story featuring Anthony and Hope.

While this was the first book of the series, the story will start with the prequel, which will be part of an anthology including 19 brand new stories from some of your favourite historical romance authors! You can preorder I Like Big Dukes and I Cannot Lie, which will be released September 12th, for only 99 cents.

And if you haven't yet signed up for my newsletter, I would love to have you join! You will receive Unmasking a Duke for free, as well as links to giveaways, sales, new releases, and stories about my coffee addiction, my struggle to keep my plants alive, and how much trouble one loveable wolf-lookalike dog can get into.

www.elliestclair.com/ellies-newsletter

Or you can join my Facebook group, Ellie St. Clair's Ever Afters, and stay in touch daily.

With love,
Ellie

The Viscount's Code
Reckless Rogues Book 2

DRAWN TOGETHER TO BREAK A CODE, **will Hope and Anthony fight for their forbidden love?**
His family name sullied after his father was branded a traitor, Anthony, Lord Whitehall, is fed up with all of the *ton*. His only allegiance is to his small group of daredevil friends, which is why he agrees to help break a code that is discovered as the next clue in their treasure hunt. The code he didn't realize he would have to break? One in the form of an angelic blond woman who sees the world in sunlight.

Lady Hope Newfield believes love is worth waiting for — it just hasn't found her yet. Then a surly viscount takes up residence at her family's country home. She cannot help the irresistible pull to him as he attempts to solve the code, despite the fact that her father has strictly forbid any connection between the viscount and his daughters.

As the hunt to break the code intensifies, so does the danger that follows them, Anthony's own search into the past, and the irresistible attraction between Hope and Anthony. Will they listen to her father and the voices of reason in their heads, or give in to all of their desires?

The second book of the Reckless Rogues series is a grumpy vs. sunshine, forbidden love, one-bed-only steamy regency romance featuring a beautiful, cheerful heroine, and a surly viscount who needs to move on from his past.

THE VISCOUNT'S CODE - CHAPTER ONE

"We cannot welcome that man into our home."

Hope bit her lip, staring up at her sister's set jaw, the hard line of her lips, the steely determination in her eyes.

"We would be doing so to help Cassandra and Gideon, Faith. It is not for ourselves."

Faith turned toward her, hands on her hips and a disapproving frown on her face. "One of these days, Hope, you will have to do start thinking of yourself instead of everyone else."

Hope sighed as she glanced across the room at Anthony Davenport, Viscount Whitehall. She agreed with her sister – she would rather not welcome to their home a man who had just called their father a thief, even if he hadn't meant for her and Faith to overhear, but to refuse would not only disappoint one of her closest friends in the world, but would also put a stall to this entire treasure hunt.

For that is what it appeared they had embarked upon – willingly or not.

"Hope, there you are." Cassandra stepped between them

and wrapped Hope's hands in her own, a warm smile on her face. "I was never able to properly thank you for all you did to bring Devon and I back together. I'm not sure that I would ever have forgiven him had you not intervened."

Heat crept up Hope's cheeks. "It was nothing, Cassandra, truly. I simply told him the truth."

"But had you not sought him out, the two of us would have been far too hard-headed to ever admit to our faults, I'm sure," Cassandra said, although the look she sent her fiancé's way was nothing but endearing. "You are quite the peacemaker."

Hope simply nodded. Cassandra was correct in that it had taken a great deal of courage for Hope to approach the earl and tell him what her friend had believed of him, but it had been tearing her apart to see Cassandra so distraught over what Hope had been sure was a misunderstanding.

Fortunately, Lord Covington, who was best friends with Cassandra's brother, Gideon, had taken her seriously and had repaired their relationship. Along the way, they had led the rest of them on a rather interesting quest which had resulted in not a treasure as expected, but rather a second clue to this puzzle that had begun at the beginning of the summer.

"Cassandra?" Hope asked now, looking around the room. It was not as though this was a great secret, as all ten of them were in on it. There were the five women whose relationship with one another had centered around their interest in reading inappropriate novels and a penchant for brandy, and the five men who, apparently, had created a club in which they sought out daring schemes and pursuits.

"Yes?" Cassandra asked, raising her eyebrows as she pushed a strand of her auburn hair back behind her ear.

"Do you truly believe the viscount is the only man who

can solve this code that appears to exist in the last clue? And are you sure it even *is* a code?"

Cassandra's initial sigh turned into a chuckle. "I am not actually certain of anything – except that the viscount seems quite convinced that the book we found will match a second, and my father was certain that your father possessed an identical volume. Do you think it will be any issue for the viscount to visit your estate?"

"I certainly think so," Faith huffed. "Do you know what he had to say about our father?"

Hope quelled her sister's words with a look, shaking her head slightly. It wouldn't do to upset Cassandra on this day that was supposed to be for her and her soon-to-be husband.

"It will be fine," she said, smoothing it all over. "Our mothers are such good friends. I should see no issue."

"Thank you," Cassandra said, relief evident on her face. "Gideon is so counting on us finding a treasure of value to restore the family's fortunes. He was utterly disappointed when the riddle we found only led to another clue, but at least it is not the end of it." She turned when her name was called from across the room.

"I best go speak to my soon-to-be mother-in-law. Thank you again for helping us in this."

As she walked away, Hope turned to her sister. "Do you see? We cannot disappoint her."

Faith sighed. "Fine. But if the viscount says anything further untoward about our family, I shall have to tell Father."

Hope cringed. Their father was not a man that many wanted to cross.

"Very well," she said, hoping the viscount would behave himself. He was rather surly, and she hadn't spent much time with him. If he did visit their estate, he would hopefully keep to himself. "Now, what do you suppose we should say to Mother to convince her to invite them?"

"Since you are so keen on this idea, I am sure you shall come up with something," Faith said primly. "You're always rather good at convincing others to do as you please, are you not?"

"Faith—"

But Faith had walked away to join their friend Madeline, leaving Hope to sigh and make her way to her mother. Faith was right. It wouldn't be difficult to put the idea into her mother's mind – she loved to show off Newfield Manor. As it happened, the estate, near the sea at Harwich, was at its very best this time of year. All Hope needed to do was convince her mother that it was her own idea. And as she was currently speaking with Lady Whitehall, it likely wouldn't take much but an innocent comment or two for the women to decide a visit was imperative.

She stole one last glance at the viscount as she walked across the room. He was cantankerous and gruff and rather scared her, though she would never admit it to anyone. Nor would she share her thoughts that he was rather handsome. Suddenly, as though he could sense her gaze, he turned and locked eyes with her – his so hard and unrelenting that she snapped her head back around as quickly as she could, running from him with an "eep!" that she hoped no one else heard.

Cassandra was wrong. She was a coward.

~~~~~

Anthony watched the angelic figure that was Hope Newfield run away from him, just like most women of her ilk were wont to do.

He scared them. He understood that and was fine with it, for he had no time to coddle a woman prone to such emotional theatrics.

If they were different people, however, the things he could do to cause that pink flush to wash over her face…. He wondered if it would travel over the rest of her body as well.

But that wasn't for him to discover. Besides, if she knew what his family was suspected of, she would want even less to do with him than she already did.

He scoffed as he turned back to Ferrington. The man would one day become a marquess, and yet he sailed through life without a care in the world, so opposite to Anthony himself, who felt the weight of it pressing on his shoulders with every step he took.

"You are to go to Newfield House, then?" Ferrington asked him, to which Anthony nodded.

"It appears so – if it can be arranged."

"Interesting," Ferrington mused, taking a sip of his drink and rocking back and forth from his toes to heels as he looked around the room. "Haven't been there in a time myself."

"Do you have reason to?" Anthony asked, picking up on something in the man's tone.

Ferrington shrugged, although the right side of his lip twitched upward. "I might have a care for a particular person there."

"Oh?" Anthony wasn't altogether interested, but it seemed liked the natural progression of the conversation.

Ferrington leaned in. "I know I shouldn't say anything, but Lady Faith has caught my eye."

"Lady Faith?" Anthony choked out. He couldn't see anything particularly attractive about the woman, who did nothing to hide the derision in her gaze every time she looked at him. He had an inkling that she believed the rumors that had followed him around.

"Yes, Lady Faith," Ferrington said dreamily before sighing

into his drink. "Unfortunately, she wants nothing to do with me."

"You asked?"

"I did. Well, asked her for a dance once or twice, to walk with me another time. She continues to turn me down."

"Why?"

Ferrington shrugged. "She will not say. She hasn't been known to be courted by any man, however, so I suppose I cannot be overly insulted."

"I see," Anthony murmured, and while he didn't care about Lady Faith's interest in a husband, he wondered if her sister felt the same about suitors. Not that it mattered to him, for he would certainly not be pursuing her.

"So how do you know about these codes?" Ferrington asked, changing the subject.

"My father taught me," Anthony said, waiting for the judgment to come, but Ferrington only seemed interested.

"How did he learn them?"

"He was a codebreaker in the war," Anthony said, wishing Ferrington would finish this line of questioning. "He had hoped I would follow him into it, but..." then all had come crashing down. "The need never arose."

"Right. Well, an interesting skill, if not one that is often required."

"True."

"Who would have thought Ashford would have need of it in some treasure hunt?" Ferrington continued.

"Who indeed."

Anthony had hoped his one-word answers would discourage Ferrington's questioning, but the man didn't seem affected by his responses at all.

"Well, best go congratulate the new couple," he said with a cheerful smile. "Best of luck with the code! We shall all be waiting to hear how you make out."

Best of luck. Anthony wished he had kept his mouth shut when he had recognized the potential of a code in the book they had unearthed. Now they were all counting on him to solve this mystery. And while he had recognized a code existed, he wasn't sure he had any chance of breaking it. He had never been nearly as intelligent as his father, unfortunately. If he was, perhaps he could have cleared his name years ago.

He watched Hope speak to her mother, who was standing with his own. Hope glanced toward him once again, and he could only imagine how much she must be regretting their agreement for him to come visit.

Anthony was rather concerned as well – for the fair Hope with her soft blonde hair, her deep blue eyes, and porcelain skin was all he had ever wanted and exactly what he couldn't have. Her beauty made Ferrington's revelation all the more surprising. What was it about Lady *Faith* that would attract a man over her sister?

Every other man he knew was enamoured with Lady Hope – a group he refused to join, as he was far from the man for her.

"Anthony!"

He had been so focused on his ridiculous musings that he hadn't been paying attention to the room around him.

"Yes, Mother?" He said when he realized she had been saying his name.

"Lady Embury has invited us to visit their estate within a fortnight."

Her mother was wringing her hands together nervously. He hated how unsure of herself she had become since their father's death and the accusations that had been brought against him.

"Would you like to accept?" he asked, even though he knew he was supposed to be encouraging the visit.

"I am not entirely sure," she said, hedging. "It would be lovely to spend time with Lady Embury. We were friends since we were girls, of course, and it has been some time since I have been to their country home. It is just…"

"Just what?"

"Since your father died, I haven't quite felt like myself."

Anthony softened at her words, and he reached out and placed a hand on her arm.

"Then perhaps a visit with an old friend is just what you need."

She hesitated before nodding, a small smile flitting across her face for just a moment.

"Perhaps you are right," she said, straightening. "I shall tell Lady Embury we will be there within a week, if you are agreeable."

"I am. I need to return home to see to a few matters, but we are in such close proximity to Newfield Manor, I see no issue."

"Wonderful!" His mother brightened, and Anthony hoped desperately that Lady Embury would be considerate and not raise any topics that would cause his mother's smile to fade. "I shall go inform her of the good news."

Anthony shoved his hands in his pockets, watching her as she returned to Lady Embury, who was standing with Lady Hope herself. Her eyes caught his once more, and he found himself nearly lost in their ocean blue depths.

"Not for me," he murmured to himself, wondering how many times in the coming days he would have to repeat that mantra. "Not for me."

* * *

Find The Viscount's Code on Amazon and in Kindle Unlimited!

ALSO BY ELLIE ST. CLAIR

The Art of Stealing a Duke's Heart

A Jewel for the Taking

A Prize Worth Fighting For

Gambling for the Lost Lord's Love

Romance of a Robbery

Thieves of Desire Box Set

The Bluestocking Scandals

Designs on a Duke

Inventing the Viscount

Discovering the Baron

The Valet Experiment

Writing the Rake

Risking the Detective

A Noble Excavation

A Gentleman of Mystery

The Bluestocking Scandals Box Set: Books 1-4

The Bluestocking Scandals Box Set: Books 5-8

Blooming Brides

A Duke for Daisy

A Marquess for Marigold

An Earl for Iris

A Viscount for Violet

The Blooming Brides Box Set: Books 1-4

Happily Ever After

The Duke She Wished For

Someday Her Duke Will Come

Once Upon a Duke's Dream

He's a Duke, But I Love Him

Loved by the Viscount

Because the Earl Loved Me

Happily Ever After Box Set Books 1-3

Happily Ever After Box Set Books 4-6

The Victorian Highlanders

Duncan's Christmas - (prequel)

<u>Callum's Vow</u>

<u>Finlay's Duty</u>

<u>Adam's Call</u>

<u>Roderick's Purpose</u>

<u>Peggy's Love</u>

<u>The Victorian Highlanders Box Set Books 1-5</u>

Searching Hearts

Duke of Christmas (prequel)

Quest of Honor

Clue of Affection

Hearts of Trust

Hope of Romance

Promise of Redemption

Searching Hearts Box Set (Books 1-5)

Christmas

Christmastide with His Countess

Her Christmas Wish

Merry Misrule

A Match Made at Christmas

A Match Made in Winter

Standalones

Always Your Love

The Stormswept Stowaway

A Touch of Temptation

For a full list of all of Ellie's books, please see
www.elliestclair.com/books.

ABOUT THE AUTHOR

Ellie has always loved reading, writing, and history. For many years she has written short stories, non-fiction, and has worked on her true love and passion -- romance novels.

In every era there is the chance for romance, and Ellie enjoys exploring many different time periods, cultures, and geographic locations. No matter when or where, love can always prevail. She has a particular soft spot for the bad boys of history, and loves a strong heroine in her stories.

Ellie and her husband love nothing more than spending time at home with their children and Husky cross. Ellie can typically be found at the lake in the summer, pushing the stroller all year round, and, of course, with her computer in her lap or a book in hand.

She also loves corresponding with readers, so be sure to contact her!

www.elliestclair.com
ellie@elliestclair.com

Ellie St. Clair's Ever Afters Facebook Group

Printed in Great Britain
by Amazon